RAIJU

A Kaiju Hunter Novel

K. H. Koehler

PROLOGUE
The End

See, the funny thing about death is that you never see it coming until it's staring you in the face. Until you're forced to look it straight in its burning red eyes. You go about your life worrying about your always-late homework, your I'll-never-get-the-nerve-to-ask-her-out, your I'm-so-gonna-fail-class-big-time, thinking it's the end of the world. At least that's how I always approached things.

Until today. Until I found myself standing in the trembling rubble that had once been New York City. The sky was inky black and choked with dust and debris, the neon lights of Times Square struggling fitfully to pierce the almost impenetrable darkness, the air full of that rotten-egg stench of open gas mains that I hated so much, and realized I was going to die today.

I watched the kaiju rise up before me, through the passage of a ripped-open manhole cover. It seemed to go on forever. Black against the black sky. Then it curled over—centipede-like, though it no longer resembled that—and stared at me with brilliant crimson eyes. It looked at me, and it looked through me, this thing that wanted to kill me, this thing that wanted me dead.

Dead, because I stood between it and the rest of humanity.

Me. Mr. Nobody.

A big part of me wanted to rage against whatever gods had conspired to bring me to this point, to end my life so callously, but I had a feeling it would do no good. I had a feeling I had always been destined to be here today, to die like this.

I raised my hands in self-defense and cried out in the last moments before the kaiju lashed out at me.

1

CHAPTER ONE
The Great American Nightmare

1

Even though I owned a bike—a nth-hand Honda VTX Cruiser that my dad helped me buy and my best friend, Wayne, helped me rebuild—my dad drove me to school that first day. I wasn't happy about that. My dad is the head cook at the Red Panda on Flatbush Avenue, and his only car is a delivery van he bought from the owner, Mr. Serizawa. I really can't think of any worse way of starting your first day at a new high school than being driven to it by your old man in a delivery van, and being Japanese made it even more clichéd.

But if it made my dad happy, I'd deal. I figured if I could get through today, I could get through just about anything.

They call this neighborhood of Brooklyn, Japantown, yet there are as many Armenian, Chinese and Indian restaurants as there are Japanese, and those open-air grocers that you think only exist in Third World countries, or on Discovery Channel specials? They line the streets up and down, but Greek and Italian families own most of them. Sure, there are plenty of Japanese in the neighborhood—like us. Many had relocated as far away from the city formerly known as San Francisco as they could without falling into the Atlantic Ocean—but I don't think the ethnic majority is in our favor. Basically, New York sucks tail.

I won't go into the whys and wherefores, but unless you've been living in a cave, I'm sure you know the story already. Monsters. Kaiju, as the top scientists studying them in Japan call them. It's all anyone wants to talk about, to study, to obsess over. You probably already have the science course at your own high school—or will, soon. Over the last few years, I've lost track of the books, magazines, and movie-of-the-week tearjerkers devoted solely to kaiju. Almost two years had passed since the day San Francisco was wiped off the map, and just like a natural disaster or a terrorist act, somehow, the horror had turned into excitement, entertainment, and science.

Me? I was there when Karkadon leveled San Francisco. I lived it. I remember every gruesome detail of the night that a monster shark ate enough polluted fish to grow a hundred times its natural size. It pulled itself from the ocean, learned to breathe air, and managed to destroy half the city before dying in a hail of military fire. Forget the blockbuster movies and sensational news reports, because I know what it was really like. I saw all the surreal nightmare stuff, the utter, crushing, finality of it all. I was going to a new school and living in a new city because of it.

Yet, if you ask anyone, they'll tell you we were one of the lucky ones. Most of my friends wound up homeless. Some of my friends didn't make it at all. I'd give anything to see them again. Hell, I'd love to see my enemies again—and they weren't exactly a joyride, if you know what I mean.

Before you continue, you should know something about me. Prior to the disaster, I was that pudgy kid with glasses who sits all alone at lunch and actually reads the books assigned to him in English class. The one that you pity, but also try to avoid, because rubbing shoulders with someone like me is like contracting a social disease. If having a genuinely awkward, unpopular, and thoroughly *unkissed* sixteen-year-old geek for a hero bothers you, I suggest you close this book immediately and move on. I won't be offended, promise. I just feel you ought to know the truth. You need to understand what I was before learning about what I've become.

A man needs to face his past before he can see his future. That's Tao, just FYI.

It started the first day of kindergarten, during recess, when all of us kids were sitting around the lunch table, naively eating our Double Stuf Oreos and slurping from our milk cartons. This kid named Bryce—who, even at the tender age of five, was built like a side of beefalo—decided I didn't look white enough. He came over and threw his milk all over me, which got a good laugh out of the rest of the kids at the table, let me tell you.

I should have slam-dunked his ass. Instead, I did the worst possible thing, the mistake that would haunt me to the end of my days in San Francisco: I told my dad. Afraid I was riding the bullet to being eternally bullied because I was only half-white, he told the principal, who immediately told Bryce's parents. You see where this is going. By the time I was in grammar school, I was known as not only a half-chink, but also a snitch and a wimp, a fantabulous trifecta of fail if ever there was one.

So, yeah, I was that kid you love to hate, tripping over outstretched legs in aisles, laughing off the abuse, and basically crying over my chocolate Ding Dongs as I played *Halo* and hoped for better days ahead. Then reality reared its ugly brute head and I learned about the days ahead. I learned about reality. I learned that revenge, even served cold, tastes awful.

Bryce died the night Karkadon came ashore. So did a lot of other kids, not all of whom had been jerks. There was Raymond, who was an even bigger egghead than I was, Wayne, the harmless stoner dude from Venice Beach who got me into bikes, and Chance, a pre-op transsexual who attracted Bryce's ire like a steel rod in a lightning storm. In fact, about half of the city's population went, including my mom, who was driving across the Golden Gate Bridge when the monster pulled it down into the San Francisco Bay.

"Looks like the squash is coming out," my dad said, looking out the window. As usual, he was thinking about the restaurant. By the way, you wouldn't think we were related. My dad is short, and he has that soft, round baby face that some Asian men carry over with them from their youth. He cooks and eats way too much. I'm as tall as a giraffe, and recently, it seems that I can't gain weight no matter how many wontons I eat.

"You know, Kevin," he said after a moment, "you don't have to go in today. Give it a few months…"

"I can't sit home all day and watch KTV," I said, then regretted it. I was being a jerk. Everyone watched the Kaiju Network these days, but hearing it run day and night at home was giving me a case of the crazies. I added, almost as an afterthought, "I've already lost almost two years of school."

"You'll make it up in no time."

Probably. I'm not a mental slouch. I just play one on television. See, the year after the kindergarten debacle, I skipped not one, but two grades. Immediately after, my mom and dad took me to an institute where they give you all kinds of tests and measure your IQ. Mine came out somewhere between genius and freak of nature. At first, I thought that was the awesomeness, but after it got me a broken nose at the end of Bryce's fist, I started to think otherwise. The obvious has never been my strong suit.

San Francisco was gone, and with it pudgy, soft, geeky, push-him-around, Kevin. In the last two years, I had grown a head taller than my dad was, and I had lost all the extra weight I'd been carrying around for years. More importantly, if you punch me, I'll punch you back.

Dad was frowning. He was worried, as usual. He works in worrying like an artist works in clay or paints. He was afraid I was going to get pushed around like in the old days. My dad's a good guy. He just didn't know that I was turning into a punk. Let's you and me keep it that way.

I reached up and fixed the shades I wear whenever I go out. I have a huge collection of them. It's something my dad picks up for me whenever he sees them, like how some girls gain those ever-expanding unicorn collections (mostly parent-started), except I'm okay with the glasses. I used to wear them back in San Francisco to hide my mom's electric blue Irish eyes in my dad's Asian face, except that now they'd become a symbol of the reborn, impervious Kevin. The ones I had chosen today were artsy, round frames with rose-tinted lenses, like something Ozzy would have worn in his trippier days. They worked great with my ragged black jeans, leather jacket, and the crazy anime hair I have that needs trimming at least once every two weeks.

"Eh, I'll be all right," I said as we pulled into the parking lot behind Thomas Jefferson High, a boxy redbrick building that looked about as friendly as a penitentiary. "It's a few fucking classes. I can handle it."

Right after San Francisco, I had developed a swearing problem. At first, my dad let it go. Then he told me to cut it out, that I sounded like a punk. He didn't say anything now. He just sat there in the parking lot, hands resting on the steering wheel of our idling, oh-so-clichéd delivery van, looking at me. He looked older, more shrunken somehow, like a turtle in a shell that wanted to draw in its head. He didn't look like my dad anymore. "Do you want me coming in, or do you want to make up an excuse?"

He and I have always been close, able to read each other's minds. He knew I wanted to go this alone, that it was important to me. But I was loathe to say that to him. He might think I didn't need him anymore.

"If you want to come in…" I shrugged, leaving it at that.

"I really want to check out that squash," he said.

He never uses squash in his stir-fry dishes.

"No problem. I'll cover you."

He slapped my knee.

I slid open the van door and jumped down with my backpack over a shoulder. "See you at four," I said.

"Can you handle registration? Do you want me to pick you up?"

"Yes to one, no to two. I don't know if there'll be an orientation or if they'll make me take tests or whatever, so lemme handle it, okay?" I shrugged. "I'll catch the bus home."

He smiled a little. "Good enough. See you at four, and good luck!"

I waved him off, feeling oddly like our roles had been reversed—like I was sending him off into unknown territory, never to return. It was a feeling that made me feel old. An old, bad fit to the school system, as if I didn't belong here. Like I just ought to take off. Yet I was just practical (or maybe stupid) enough, to turn around and start toward the building anyway.

As things turned out, it was that great and wonderful practicality of mine which changed my life forever.

2

I felt a childish stab of nervous energy as I headed for the school.

Kids were climbing the steps, shoving each other, catcalling, referencing games I hadn't seen and teams I didn't know. They all looked like they fit together. They had that perfect cohesion you only see with kids who grew up together in the same neighborhood. New York kids. A tough crowd. I thought about metal detectors at the doors, cops in the hallways, guns in lockers. I wondered if all the horror stories I'd heard were true.

Gradually I picked out the various cliques: skinny jeans and reversible jackets on the skate guys, a few tough-looking pusher types at the fence, some stoner dudes trudging around in their own little circles, and the jocks jaunting around sans jackets to show off all their gym muscle. Geeks and Emos on the fringes. Don't think generalizations stand true? You haven't been in high school of late. The girls looked pretty normal in jeans and tees, or those short plaid skirts and funky jumper dresses that were all the rage—except, as usual, the cheerleaders had *way* more energy than anyone should at this ungodly hour.

I squinted at the bright sunshiny sky, hating it, wanting it to rain, feeling old, feeling like I needed more coffee, a cigarette, or something. For the hundredth time that morning, I wished I had my bike. At least, if I screwed up so badly I couldn't show my face around here anymore, I'd have an escape route. As it was, I was stuck here till four. Can you say groan?

There were, of course, bullies. A couple of big ones in varsity jackets were loitering at the doors, doing what bullies do, eyeing up the girls like they were the daily specials and making obnoxious comments in the direction of the pansier-looking boys. No matter where you go, a bully is a bully, and they all came from the same Bryce-mold, it seems, created in the same alien Bryce-universe.

I realized I had to get up the stairs and through the front doors, and still, somehow, remain invisible, and the next few seconds were critical. I regretted wearing the shades. If the bullies spotted them, they might peg me as a hippie tree-hugger, which would probably get me killed in this school. So I lowered my head slightly, so that my jawcut hair flopped forward to either side of my face like a curtain, and started climbing the steps casual-fast.

A small group of kids in black fishnet and leather were going in ahead of me, making scary faces at everyone. Maybe, I thought, they would be enough of a distraction that the evil bully-force from the evil bully galactic empire would never notice me. I could dream, anyway. I slipped in ahead of the skate guys and took up my place behind the group in black. I saw funky short funeral dresses on the girls, and outrageous black poet shirts and chain jeans on the guys. *What an eclectic mix*, I thought. *We even have Goths.*

Well, it turns out that New York produces an even meaner bunch of kids than I was used to, because one of the bullies stuck out his foot, tripping up the Goth girl in the lead. That annoyed me. Not the foot-thing (that's an ancient tactic that's whispered around primitive fires on Planet Bully), but the fact that he was going after a girl. Even Bryce and his band of Troglodytes wouldn't have tried that shit. I mean, come on, weren't there any rules or codes of honor on Planet Bully, however unfair and haphazard?

I saw it happen. I didn't think much about it. I dropped my pack, reached through the wall of taffeta and lace, and caught the girl at the elbow, steadying her on her monster plats. She was tiny and it was a long way down the school steps. She would have achieved freefall longer than a military paratrooper. She fell back against me, catching my toe under her heel, which hurt like hell, but right then, I was too pissed about the lack of rules to notice the pain.

"Dayum," said the bully who had tripped the girl. He was huge, hulking, and fingering his football letter-jacket to emphasize his jockness, even though it had probably been bought on sale by his mommy. "Hey, Zack, man, look at this. The Goths are multiplying now."

Zack, the other jerk blocking the door like a muscle-bound gargoyle, sniggered as if his friend was a regular cut-up. It never fails to amaze me what kinds of kindergarten humor amuses these types. I'm pretty sure most of them were deprived of oxygen at a critical point in their development, or dropped on their heads in the delivery room.

I stood there and glared at the first bully, the one I had mentally tagged "The Hulk." "You wanna tell your brain dead buddy to move before I do some *multiplication* on his face?"

Yeah, it shocked me too. It just popped out of my big fat mouth, and I felt a strange commingling of pride, arrogance, sweating, and heart-rending fear. It was kind of like swatting a wasps' nest with a stick, just to see if you can outrun the wasps. Except I wasn't running.

"You little fuck!" The Hulk growled. "I'd like to see you fucking try it!"

Pro tip: Bullies use a lot of unnecessary swear words just to show you how big and tough they are, and often enough, they shout them, like you're completely deaf. We eyed each other for a cold, brief moment, like gunslingers in a spaghetti western, waiting for the other one to go for his six-shooter. When his little show of testosterone garnered no reaction from me, he lunged forward and grabbed at the front of my jacket.

So I did what any normal, pissed-off punk would do. I punched him square in the nose.

3

So much for staying invisible, I thought ten minutes later.

The Vice Principal of Thomas Jefferson High—a frighteningly overweight, middle-aged woman with a face that could have stopped a fleet of trucks—glared at me accusingly, and I looked blankly back at her with a *Who, me? I'm innocent* look on my face. This was my first time IDS (In Deep Shit), so it was a new experience for me. I didn't know what to expect.

I glanced around the front office, at the cheery potted plants, the motivational posters that obviously came from some other universe where everything was butterflies and unicorns, and the VP that was seriously creeping me out. I wasn't sure what was more useless, trying not to concentrate on the constellation of moles on her face, or trying not to squirm around on the ultra-hard plastic Chair of Doom. Every school has one, and all of them are hard and cold for the hard, cold criminal sitting in them, waiting for sentencing to be passed.

"Mr. Takahashi," said the VP (making my name sound like a disease recently discovered to have the viral capacity to wipe out small continents), "we do have counselors here at TJ High to address the troubles of our at-risk students, and we feel that you might benefit from..."

I tuned out her buttery-soft voice, which was completely at odds with her appearance; she wasn't fooling anyone. She was wearing a dark, tight pea-green suit that positively screamed, *I am the warden of this teen penitentiary and I will whip you with chains like Ilsa, She Wolf of the SS!* Unfortunately, she looked nothing like the actress who played Ilsa (who is a total hottie—not that I would know anything about that). She did keep rubbing at the mondo-nasty mole growing on her upper lip. I thought the woman must weigh a metric ton, a lot of it pure muscle. I imagined her flinging metal protractors ninja-style at troublesome kids from down the hallway.

"Mr. Takahashi...?"

My attention snapped away from the nameplate on the desk that read Ms. Cinnamon, VP. I was willing to bet she was made of anything but sugar and spice—and I centered it instead on her face, which reminded me of Boris Karloff, just not that attractive. "Yeah," I said, trying desperately to backtrack and figure out what she was saying. "Yes, Ms. Cinnamon."

There was a derisive glint in the woman's evil yellow eyes as she pawed around her desk drawers for a class schedule and the rulebook. I was another wounded refugee from the West Coast, here to clutter the halls and infest her school with my own particular brand of bohemian San Francisco mayhem. She rather haphazardly marked my classes for me, gave me a padlock to a locker, then handed me a student rules handbook and a brochure with a happy, smiling rainbow face on it that read, *Managing Your Anger the Right Way!*

Seriously, was she for real?

"We're going to forego calling your father this time, Mr. Takahashi, but only because this is your first day with us," Ilsa the She Wolf said as if she were doing me a huge favor. "However, should Troy decide to submit a complaint, we may need to re-address this issue in the future."

I didn't think that was going to be a problem. After I punched Troy (a.k.a., The Hulk) in the face, he staggered around in a circle with tears in his eyes, using both hands to cover the nose-leak I'd given him. He'd looked shocked and hurt; it was probably the first time anyone had ever hit him, including his parents. I had waited, fists clenched and upraised, for him to retaliate, but he and his brainless lackey suddenly turned tail and raced down the steps of the school like the hounds of hell were at their heels, Troy leaking blood the whole way. If I knew bullies, and I thought I did, Troy wouldn't be making a big issue out of this, especially since half the school had witnessed him crying like a dorky five-year-old girl who'd skinned her knee.

"Are you listening to me, Mr. Takahashi?"

"Absolutely, Ms. Ilsa." *Oops.*

Ms. Cinnamon looked like she wanted to slap the yellow off me. In retrospect, this probably wasn't the best way to introduce myself to a new school. She narrowed her wolfish eyes and said, "You are dismissed...for now, but I will be watching, Mr. Takahashi, you can be sure of that."

"Thank you, Ms. Cinnamon!" I grabbed my backpack and scrambled my way out of that office. I was so relieved that I was out of there that I wasn't watching where I was going and nearly collided with a girl standing just outside the office door.

"Hi," she said, stepping back to give me room. Her voice was soft, breathy, and like the rest of her, it froze me solid in my tracks.

I stared with surprise at the pale, dark-haired, Gothic girl I had rescued from Troy's evil machinations, and gave her a quick once-over. She definitely had some Japanese in her. I saw that at once. She stood there in her glittering black clothes and geisha whiteface, watching me shyly from behind the short stack of books in her arms. The air between us became electric; no lie. I had a moment when I felt I knew her from somewhere, as if we were connected in some way. It was a weird feeling.

Then I shook my head to clear it, and the moment passed. "Um...hi." I glanced back at the closed office door. "You're not...um, next, are you?"

As you can tell, I'm not my articulate best standing before ultra-hot chicks.

She narrowed her exquisitely painted eyes and tilted her head so her purple-streaked pigtails were crooked. She looked as if she, too, had experienced that sudden strangeness. "No...I cut homeroom. I just wanted to see you, to thank you for before. That was really great of you," she said, blinking in a totally seductive way. "Taking care of Troy, I mean."

"No problem," I said, trying to sound casual about it, like I did this every day. Kevin Takahashi: Savior of Gothic Girls Everywhere.

We instinctively moved away from the danger of the front office and down the empty hallway. Slowly, the familiar school smells of chalk dust, books, and industrial cleaner closed in around us—it wasn't great stuff, but anything was better than the stinky potpourri smell of the VP's office. The girl narrowed her eyes with concern. "Did you get in deep with the Cinnamonster?" she asked.

I tried to answer but I had something that felt like a walnut stuck in my throat. I mean, the Gothic girl was beyond beautiful—glamorous, surreal, like a teen actress on the WB. It took me two whole tries before I was able to get the words out. "Nah," I finally answered, trying to play it off like nothing, and proud of the fact that I wasn't stuttering anymore like a moron. "I'm cool, but...the Cinnamonster? I mean, is she for real? I just kept staring, and..."

Real slick, I thought, and decided to shut up before I made a total fool of myself.

Her black eyes blinked up at me, and her lips, painted a moist, glittering sapphire, turned up at the corners as if she found me amusing. I felt my ears burning and I wanted to die—or, at least, melt through the floor and out of sight. "Yep, that's our Cinnamonster, and believe it or not, she's for real. The council is still out on what planet she's from, though. Most of us think Uranus."

I laughed at that.

"I'm Aimi Mura," she said as she stopped to face me. "That's Aimi with two I's."

It took me a moment to catch on—I wasn't used to girls who looked like Aimi talking to me. I wanted to look around the empty school halls to see if she was addressing some other dude. I mean, sure, I'd gone out on a handful of dates, but they were always "study dates" at the local library with fat, desperate chicks that I had nothing in common with.

"Kevin," I finally muttered, "with one." I was starting to think my truncated responses were making me sound mentally-deficient, so I added "Takahashi," like my fantabulous, non-American, utterly un-apple pie, impossible-to-spell surname should impress her.

Evidently, it did. "Kevin Takahashi-san," she said as if she was tasting my name. She dipped her head in a little formal bow and said something in Japanese that I didn't understand at all.

I shook my head in confusion; I'd never had much interest in my dad's native language. So Aimi leaned in close to whisper to me, which was totally worth not knowing Japanese, because I got a whiff of her dark chocolaty-cherry perfume. "I said…Troy is going to be majorly pissed with you tomorrow."

"No problem," I repeated. "I can handle him." Worried? Who, me?

"You're very brave, Kevin," said Aimi, shifting her books around in her arms. The lace of her dress made hissing noises as it rubbed together, which was kind of distracting.

"Not really. I mean…um…thanks."

"And really *kawaii*…that means cute." She kept staring at me in a totally absorbed way.

Finally, completely embarrassed by her scrutiny, I looked around at the posters and activity boards with paper fall leaves stapled to them like they were the most amazing things I had ever seen. Bullies? No problem, but pretty girls were impossible for me to look in the eye.

I was literally saved by the bell—a nasally, impatient noise that made us both jump in the moments before the doors of all the homeroom classrooms opened up, dumping their load of students into the hallway of the school. My brain and body rebelled. Was I really clamming up in the face of a gorgeous girl who wanted to talk to me? Was I really this lame?

Evidently so. It should have been awesome. Every guy's dream to have a fantastic girl like Aimi talking to him. Instead, it made me feel sad and anxious in a way I had never felt with any of the fat, desperate chicks.

"Kevin," she said, and I finally looked at her. "*Domo arigato.* That means thank you. For everything."

"Okay."

I saw her little clique of Goths zeroing in on her through the sea of students. As they moved to surround her like a small, impenetrable army, she added, "Maybe I'll see you around?"

"Sure."

Of course not. I had no idea why she was still talking to me when it was obvious that I was a complete loser. Still smiling, she waved to me in the moments before her friends swept her away.

I didn't wave back. Instead, I turned and hurried down the hall in some random direction. I felt Aimi's eyes on my back the whole way, but I didn't look back. She was just being polite. Nice to the new kid who had helped her out.

I almost hoped it was true, because I was much too afraid to imagine otherwise.

4

After Troy, the Cinnamonster, and then making a fool of myself in front of Aimi Mura, I expected the rest of my morning to go downhill fast, but Algebra II went easily enough. The room was big, the desks rawboned with age, the environment of squeaking chalk on blackboards, and the smell of old books and school disinfectant all too familiar. Best of all, the students were busy with a pop quiz when I finally found it.

The teacher, Mr. Russo, was a young guy who couldn't be more than a year out of college, but had somehow managed to go all grey. He shook my hand, gave me a textbook, and then sent me to an empty desk in the back corner of the room. My hero.

For the next half hour, I kept my head down and listened to the busy scritch of pencils on paper. Aimi wasn't here, and neither were any of her Goth friends. I wondered if I would see her later today. I wondered if we shared any classes. I paged idly through the textbook, which looked about as challenging as a first-grade reader. At least I'd be able to ace the tests without having to study or even pay much attention in class.

Unfortunately, Algebra II gave me false hope in the Remaining Invisible department, because when I got to Biology, Mrs. Rodriguez pointed me out to everyone in class and asked me how I liked New York, like I had a choice being here. Even worse, it turned out the class was studying Introduction to Kaijuology. I knew right then and there that Mrs. Rodriguez and I would never be friends.

In Latin class, a tall, chunky Hispanic girl with wild red hair sat next to me, then followed a few tentative steps behind me in the halls before speaking up. "You're Kyle, right?" she said. Unlike most of the girls with their designer teen wardrobes, she was dressed tomboyishly in distressed jeans and an element vest over a button down chambray shirt. I had no idea if she was trying to hide her extra weight or if that was just her style—and not much interest in finding out right at the moment.

"Kevin," I said, sticking my hands deep in my pockets as I ambled along. I was trying to ignore the fact that a couple of girls were standing at their lockers, laughing about me behind their phones.

"I heard you gave Troy a broken nose, his first," she said. She sounded pleased. I noticed she walked with a lot of confidence for a big girl. "No one's ever stood up to him before."

"Really?" I said, trying not to sound too crabby and failing miserably. "And I thought this school was full of wannabe gangstas."

She gave me a challenging look, like it would take a lot more than a scowling Kevin Takahashi and a few insults to chase her off. "Don't believe all the ghetto movies. We don't boost cars or knock over convenient stores—at least, most of us don't. My name's Michelle." She smiled broadly. She had clean but crooked teeth, and her nails were rimmed with work grease. She so wasn't Aimi—was almost the antithesis of Aimi in every way—All-American, imperfect, girl-next-door, whatever you wanted to call it. Then I wondered why I was comparing the two of them like that, and felt a little ashamed. It wasn't like Aimi was ever likely to talk to me again after I ran away from her.

I had Michelle in English too, and as we made our way to the cafeteria at lunch, she took great pains to warn me about the free school lunch, the horror of which would haunt me forevermore. I had to give her points, because she wasn't at all deterred by my sulking or silence. She went on about her friends and what teachers she hated and her dad who ran a custom body shop in the

Heights. She said she helped him out on the weekends. A girl who liked cars. Who woulda thunk it?

We sat near the windows and she introduced me to her "little" brother, Terry, who, despite being a freshman, was allowed to sit at the sophomore table. Mostly, I think, because anyone who challenged Michelle was likely to get smacked. Michelle told me not to mind Terry, since the doctors had dropped him on his head as a baby.

Terry was huge, bespeckled, and actually had the guts to wear a Star Trek TOS tunic to school and a belt that contained just about every imaginable Radio Shack device you could imagine, which made me want to run screaming from the school. I had hoped to avoid the whole geek squad entirely, but it seemed they were determined to suck me in no matter what I did. I thought about changing tables, but every table in the cafeteria was occupied by a clique that I was not a part of.

With a mental sigh (which is harder to do than it sounds), I turned my attention on the bench against the back wall, just under the bell, where a bunch of guys and girls in black were slowly amassing like a long row of human-size crows in fluffy black lace. I assumed this was the outlaw bench, the place where the weird and unwanted perched. Like the Chair of Doom, there's one in every school.

I spotted Aimi immediately. Beside her were the other Goths, three boys and one girl. Two of the guys were African-American—twins, I think—with coordinating tuxedoes and Baron Samedi makeup. The other one was white, and dressed in a black priest's cassock, with a froth of lace at his throat and cuffs. Somehow, he managed to stand out even more than the twins, partly because he was one of the few all-white guys at school, mostly because he wore his bone-white hair down to his shoulders, and his face powdered as pale as a corpse. I think he was looking for an elegant, almost effeminate Gothic look, but he had the naturally muscled body of a track-and-field guy, and looked like he could put another guy his size through a brick wall, especially if they made fun of his fancy outfit. His attention was riveted on Aimi, hanging on every word she said. Ugh.

Aimi didn't seem to notice, though, engaged as she was in a lively debate with the other Goth girl—an Indian girl with fiery red, Raggedy Anne dreads and a frilly black dress. I stared longer than was appropriate. Aimi was explaining something to Raggedy Anne on a sheet of music paper. None of them seemed to be eating. All of them wore more powder and makeup than an '80's hair metal band. With the exception of the white-haired dude, I wondered how they managed to survive in this school.

Michelle noticed my looking. "Don't even bother with them," she said with authority. "They're weird." She bit savagely into her Snickers bar. "You hang with them, you'll look like them. Like Snowman."

"Snowman was sooo pissed this morning that he almost punched out the Cinnamonster when she caught him smoking in the bathroom!" Terry informed us. He grinned hugely as he jiggled his fat in his seat, and worked a travel screwdriver into some poor little device laid out in pieces in front of him. I think it had once been a PDA.

"What happened? Did his hair not come out right today?" Michelle asked cattily. "Or is his corset too tight?"

Terry made deep rumbling sounds that reminded me uncomfortably of Fat Albert laughing. "He wanted to be the one to knock Troy's lights out this morning when he messed with Aimi, but then Kevin…"

"Snowman?" I interrupted them, looking at the white guy. I thought I hadn't heard right. "You must be kidding me."

"I wish."

I looked back at the Goths, Snowman in particular. He looked about as friendly as the plague. "How do they get away with, you know…" I waved my hand at the wall of black clothes and spiky, multicolored hair.

"Looking like freaks and not being skinned, gutted, and hung over a fence by Troy and his fathead football friends?" Michelle finished (I thought rather colorfully) for me. She seemed to be an authority on everything at TJ High. "They play The Hole on weekends. It's this dump all the losers hang out at in the Bronx. They take donations for refugees from the West Coast, bring in a lot of money, or so I hear, so they can dress anyway they want."

"So they're allowed to dress like that to promote the band," I guessed.

"The teachers are down with it. And anyway, it's Aimi's band, and no one tells Aimi what to do. If they did, her dad would just get them fired."

"I don't get it."

"Her dad's got *mucho dinero*," Michelle explained while rubbing her first and second fingers together. "He's Dr. Mura...you know, head honcho of MuraTech?"

I blinked in amazement. I was certainly familiar with the name. MuraTech is one of the biggest corporations in the world, involved in water treatment plants and in cleaning up toxic chemical spills. You hear the name everywhere you go, even if you're not a science geek. There are always news articles about the company in magazines and on TV, stuff about MuraTech vacuuming up oil spills off the coast of Alaska and generally promoting better living through green energy. As far as I knew, MuraTech was still mopping up the mess left behind by Karkadon. Not that I was going to let on that I knew that much. If I read Wired and Scientific American, Michelle didn't need to know about it.

"If Aimi's all moneyed up, why's she going here?" I said, glancing around the green cinderblock walls and dingy grey-tiled floors. I mean, Thomas Jefferson High looked like a prison both inside and out, not the type of place a girl like Aimi was likely to attend. "This place isn't exactly Beardsley."

"She was going to Beardsley." Michelle rolled her eyes with just a hint of massive jealousy. "They threw her out after she displayed uncouth and generally slutty behavior. TJ High is the end of the road for Aimi before military school...or a juvie detention center."

I found that just a little hard to believe. Aimi hadn't struck me as your typical poor little rich-girl Paris Hilton-type on the easy road to self-destruction. Back in San Francisco, before the disaster, my mom and dad had worked as a catering team and had done tons of rich-kid-slash-celebrity parties. I knew what rich kids were all about. I made a point to avoid them.

I noticed that "Snowman" was looking my way, beady little blue eyes set fast on me like he just knew I was talking about Aimi. Great. I hadn't even made it through my first day and it looked like I was about to experience *The Bully Brigade 2: The Sequel.*

"I wonder how she got like that," I said. "It takes a lot to change a person. She probably didn't start out that way."

"Who knows," said Michelle, peeling the wrapper off her second candy bar. "Who cares?"

I didn't know if I liked Michelle any better than Snowman. Obviously, Michelle's group and Aimi's band hated on each other big time. *Just what I needed,* I thought, *turf warfare.*

"Oh man, oh man, oh man!" Terry said, dropping his screwdriver and trying in vain to slink down in his seat, though he only managed to push his fat around in the seat.

I didn't think something like this would actually happen on my first day, but Snowman got to his feet and started approaching our table. He had nerve, I'd give him that. Both Michelle and Terry leaned back in their seats, appreciating what they no doubt anticipated was an exciting floorshow.

Snowman stopped at our table and stared down at me. He was big. Bigger than most of the teachers here. Maybe bigger than me. His gestures up until now had been fluid and overly elegant, like something he practiced in a mirror at home. Now he just looked like any other punk spoiling for a fight.

Michelle glanced up with catty eyes. "Like the coat, Snow. What time's the funeral?"

Snowman smirked. "Like yours better, Michelle. It's so butch, so totally you." Before Michelle could respond, he turned his diamond-hard, laser-powered eyes on me. "Kenny, right?" His voice was rough, like someone with a perpetual cold.

It made me want to clear my throat. "Kevin," I corrected him, trying to sound as neutral as possible. "What can I do for you, chief?"

"Can I speak with you in private?" His eyes lit over the table, nothing in them even remotely friendly. "Away from all the...ladies."

I looked past his big frame to the rest of the Goths. Aimi was on her feet, hovering undecidedly, but I didn't want to signal to her. I figured I didn't need to involve her anymore in this than she already was.

Instead, I returned my attention to Snowman. "Sure. Why not?" Because if we had to clear the air, why not do it as soon as possible? I mean, he couldn't be any tougher than Troy.

Could he?

5

I tried to ignore the three hundred-plus pairs of student eyes that followed us out of the lunchroom, to no avail. I was probably going to make school history—again.

I thought we were going to step outside behind the school, where the traditional beat-downs always take place, but when we had reached the end of the hallway where the boy's washroom was located, Snowman pushed the door open for me. I hesitated, recalling all the stupid action flicks I'd seen where the hit man takes out victims in the john. Then I kicked myself mentally. He was just a kid. He was tough, but I was tougher. I ducked under his arm and stepped into the washroom.

Snowman waited until the door had swung shut mechanically behind us before he started sizing me up. "So you're the hothead who punched Troy's lights out." He looked me up and down like he didn't believe my skinny ass was capable of it.

"I guess so."

"And you've met Aimi." He smirked, not a happy look.

I stood my ground, met his even gaze. I had guessed right. We were about the same size, which was saying a lot. He was more muscular, but I could hold my own. "Yeah," I responded, trying to stay cool-headed. "I've met her."

"You talked to her this morning."

I gave him a cocky look. I wasn't aware that Snowman was Aimi's PR manager, or that I had to make an appointment. "I talked to a lot of kids this morning. What's your point, chief?"

"There are rules here," he said.

"Rules. Really?"

"Really," he drawled. "Rule One: you don't mess with my crew. Rule Two: Aimi is my crew."

"Brilliant," I said.

He narrowed his eyes. "She's a very special girl," he said, "very different."

"Translation: you're insecure and you think she's stupid."

He let out his breath as if he was exasperated with me, turned sharply, and punched in one of the stall doors. His fist left a mark. It was supposed to frighten me. It did.

I thought about what Michelle had said about Snowman taking on the Cinnamonster. I guess, like Troy, he was used to getting what he wanted around these parts. Unfortunately for Troy, he was home sucking Campbell's chicken broth through a straw.

"I've known Aimi for a while," Snowman stated in a menacing tone. "She has a lot of problems she's dealing with right now. She's not well, and she's not ready for you." He took a step toward me.

Oh, he so wasn't crossing the line into my personal space. He so wasn't going there.

"Maybe that's for Aimi to decide," I said. "What are you, her therapist?"

He glared at me. "I'm her best friend."

I glared back. "Well, best friend, I didn't see your sorry ass jumping in to fight Troy this morning. Were you asleep?"

Suddenly, he was up against me, pushing me skirmish-style, the line forgotten. It wasn't a hard push. It was meant to prove a point, not inflict real damage, but he was a strong bastard and it knocked me against a towel dispenser, the impact dislodging my sunglasses before I could catch them.

I waited for him to say something snarky about my eyes, or to go for me like Troy had, but we ended up just staring at each other and doing the spaghetti western thing again.

Finally, he let out his breath. "You don't understand anything about Aimi. Just leave her alone. Consider this a warning…your first and last." He turned away and stormed out of the washroom, slamming the door behind him.

I let out my breath. He was warning *me*? I swore. I kicked in a stall door, but I didn't feel any better.

Two fights. On my first day. I was so batting zero. I could just hear my dad laying into me if I wound up in detention. He really would think I'd turned into a punk. *Then again,* I thought as I picked up my glasses and exited the washroom just in time for the bell, *maybe, at last, I had.*

6

I managed not to get into any more fights for the rest of the day. Go, me.

I muddled through Computer Lab, then PE, which I loathe with a passion born of pain. Coach Kuznik was teaching wrestling, which made things even worse. There's nothing like experiencing some sweaty guy's BO up close and personal, and it can drop you in your tracks, I swear. *I should just kill myself now,* I thought, but Shop was the last class of the day.

I usually love Shop—it's the only class I really pay attention to anymore—but I just drifted through it, distracted by what had happened back in the boy's washroom. I barely noticed that Michelle was in my class and was trying to make eye contact with me the whole time. I couldn't help it. My head was back there, confronting Snowman, and running a bunch of useless alternate scenarios through my head. Things like I should have knocked his teeth out, or I should have laughed it off and just walked out. Too late now.

Maybe my dad was right, I thought. *Maybe this was a mistake. Maybe I ought to just get the hell out of Dodge.* I was seriously considering it while threading my way back to my locker after last bell, but when I got there, I found a note that someone had slipped through the grates of my locker. It was written on fancy, cream-colored notebook paper and read:

Dear Kevin,
Sorry about what happened with Snowman. He can be a big jerk, but you probably already know that. Maybe you'll come see us play at The Hole this Friday? (I'll tell Snow to behave.) I'm in a band. It's not big (yet) but maybe one day.
I look forward to seeing you again.
Aimi

PS – Maybe you'd like to learn more Japanese words? Anata ga daisuki – *that means I really like you.*

I noticed a couple of things right away: the paper smelled like Aimi's perfume and she had dotted all her I's with those little hearts. I didn't know if that was significant. Maybe it just meant that she'd been really bored when she was writing it.

Don't laugh. Girls have it so easy. They just have to sit and wait for the guy they like to ask them out. Guys, on the other hand, have to do all the work and figure out all the signals, and we don't get a girl-body-language manual to help us out, either.

I picked up my pack and slammed my locker closed, still studying the letter.

Across the hall I spotted Vice Principal Cinnamon, a.k.a., The Cinnamonster, standing like a dour sentinel under the bell, arms crossed, clicking a staple gun threateningly, while she eyed all the students racing by. I could almost see her categorizing them as they passed—class-cutter, smoker, cheater, stoner, etc. She gave me a once-over, then narrowed her evil little reptilian eyes like she was trying to stuff me into all of those categories at once. I so didn't need Meisterfrau Ilsa on my ass. I quickly slipped out the rear exit that led to the student parking lot behind the school.

Out in the chilly October sunshine, the buses were pulling out like a herd of hissing dragons. There were a few tough pusher-types smoking near the chain link fence, and a bunch of skate guys who had gathered to rocket race each other on homemade U-ramps made of plywood.

I immediately spotted Snowman. He was hard to miss. He was leaning against the low stone wall that encircled the back lot, talking and smoking cloves, and being all clichéd with his band of un-merry Goths, Aimi among them. She noticed me at once and gave me a shy little wave.

I thought about waving back, but I knew that I would only draw Snowman's ire. Instead, my eyes shifted to a black van parked by the wall with the emblazoned word DESTROYER painted on its side, in crazy fire-red gradient paint. I wondered if that was the band's van. I wondered if Snowman had come up with such a lame-ass name.

Mr. Tall, Dark, and Gloomy, noticed me anyway. He took a long drag on his cigarette, dropped it, and crushed it under his boot heel like a gangster in a turf war movie. Then he hung his arm over Aimi's shoulder, challenging me to do something about it.

"Man," I said to myself, "you are so dead, I don't know why you bothered to be born at all." I flipped him the bird.

He pushed himself off the wall, but one of the skate guys cut between us. I took the opportunity to jump aboard the nearest bus, making the decision to stick with the school if for no other reason than because my presence seemed to thoroughly piss him off. Pissing off Snowman was going to be my new favorite hobby.

7

When I got home, I immediately went upstairs to the loft we rent from Mr. Serizawa. It's rough, barely habitable, really—a converted attic space with brownstone walls and a slanted roof that makes me stoop to see out the windows. It's better than the projects, which house two, sometimes three, families per flat since the disaster. I changed into my uniform and spent the rest of the afternoon in the restaurant downstairs, bussing tables, taking take-out orders and going through the long list of dinner specials.

I like the work, and it keeps that part of my brain that wants to dwell on everything else nicely deactivated. I don't have to think, just do, but around eight o'clock, my dad emerged from the kitchen in his grease-stained cook's whites, stinking of soy sauce and peanut grease, to tell me the late-shift guys were coming in and I could do what I wanted—which meant, in Dad-speak: "Go do your homework."

I stayed on, doing dishes, way too amped to look at textbooks until well after ten, when my dad finally chased me out of the kitchen and told me to go check on Groucho. I gave in this time. I was tired, emotionally wiped from the day, and the incessant background noise of KTV was starting to get to me.

My dad likes to keep the TV running in the kitchen night and day. I think he's afraid of being caught out unprepared should another Karkadon make landfall. Between you and me, I hate the Kaiju Channel. I hate the sensational news reports and the elaborate searches for the Chupacabra and Nessie that never come to anything. With the Karkadon dead, there was no new news to report. Documentaries and reality television shows had cropped up to fill in the empty time slots, and they sucked on so many levels. You can only interview people who saw the monster firsthand so many times before it all starts to blur together, before you start going numb.

Yet, people continue to watch KTV as avidly as CNN after 9/11, afraid, much like my dad, of being blindsided by disaster. When I consider what happened to San Francisco, the extent of the damage, I wonder if any kind of advance warning would have been enough. Somehow, I doubt it. You can predict earthquakes and typhoons, but you just can't anticipate monsters.

It started to rain while I was outside walking Groucho. Groucho is Mr. Serizawa's Rottweiler, bought for security reasons, except he's afraid of sirens, storms, water, bright lights, and everything that breathes oxygen. On the upside, you never have to wait very long for him to do his business, because he's terrified of the cats that scrounge around in the alley behind the restaurant. "This is like a country-western song," I told Groucho. "Standing in the rain, under her window, thinking about her...except I don't know where in the city her window is."

"Baroo?" Groucho said nervously. He'd heard some rats fighting over a burger wrapper in the shadows at the back of the alley. In Groucho's defense, the rats here are huge, probably because they eat the radioactive danger dogs off the sidewalk vendor's carts. After a while, we went back inside and Groucho followed me up to my room. He sleeps with me because I keep a light on at night and he's afraid of the dark.

I spent a long time just lying in bed, reading through Pat Frank's *Alas, Babylon*, and listening to the rain pinging off the roof like BBs. Generally speaking, I can usually chunk out a 400-page epic in one sitting. It's not something I like to admit to, but neither is it something I'm willing to give up. In fact, it's the only thing about the old Kevin that I've hung onto. Tonight, I was seriously distracted, as I found myself thinking about Aimi and school and New York. Everything and nothing in particular. How crazy the world was. How the world was this one thing before

Karkadon pulled itself ashore, and how it became something else afterward. Crazy stuff.

Eventually, I fell into a light sleep—the only sleep I experience anymore. Sometime in the night, I had one of those long, involved dreams that leave you feeling exhausted and vaguely troubled the next morning.

Usually, I dream about Karkadon. I dream about the night it came ashore. I dream I'm trying to phone my mom about the news report on the TV. Her cell phone rings and rings, but I never get through. No one ever picks up—because my mom's car was already at the bottom of the Bay.

Tonight, though, I dreamed I was back in the library at my old school in San Francisco, except that Aimi was there, too. I guess we were having a study date or something because she said, "Maybe you'd like to learn more Japanese words?" and I said, "Yes." So she started reading a book to me, but not in English. After a while, I took it from her and glanced at the pages. They were covered up and down in Japanese kanji characters. I don't know kanji, or even katakana, which is informal kanji, but, somehow, I could read this.

My lips started to move as I read down the page, but suddenly Aimi leaned forward and touched my lips with two of her fingertips, hushing me. "Don't, Kevin! Don't say her name. She wakes." Then she started to cry.

I looked up to say I'm sorry, but Aimi was gone, and sitting across from me was the most beautiful Asian woman I had ever seen. Her face was milk white, her lips fire red, and all of her was framed in blood red ropes of hair that almost seemed alive. She was clearly Japanese, but her eyes were as blue as mine, as blue as my mom's had been. She smirked at me, a knowing look, and her teeth were very white and very sharp in her mouth.

"Who?" I asked the woman, standing up. "Who wakes?" Suddenly, it was very important to me.

Flames suddenly sprang up from the book on the table in front of me, burning a name in the fragile rice pages.

The name was RAIJU.

Then I woke up.

CHAPTER TWO
Thunder Underground

1

"Kev! Coffee's on!" Dad called from the kitchen where he was, even at this ungodly hour, already rattling around.

What a night. I felt all banged up getting out of bed, like I'd fought a war, and the bedclothes were so tangled that I figured I must have lost that war.

What a strange dream. I kept thinking about it as I climbed out of bed.

The rain had stopped and all I could hear was the despondent drip-drip off the gutters outside, dishes clattering together in the kitchen, and the drone of the TV going. "Be right there," I said, or gargled. I am so not a morning person.

My bedroom faces east, so the sun always hits me right in the face if I oversleep, even through the mesh industrial windows. We're a blue-collar working family, and I can't remember the last time the sun beat me to rising. It's black when I go to bed and black when I get up, even on the weekends.

I showered and dressed, choosing a black Nehru shirt I left untucked and a pair of faded black jeans with the knees ripped out. I wasn't trying to be haute couture, but when you do your shopping at the Salvation Army, you take what you can get. The black suited me, made me look even bigger than I was. Maybe Snowman would challenge me today, maybe not. Either way, I was going in fighting. I sighed, hooked my damp hair behind my ear, and sat down on the closed lid of the toilet to smoke my morning cigarette with the bathroom window open.

I was so lost in thought that I almost didn't feel the floor quivering. I heard the soap dish rattle against the vanity and slowly got to my feet, while most of my internal organs sank so far down they might as well have taken refuge in my big clunky biker boots. My first thought was, *It's back. The thing. Karkadon.* Then I remembered how dead it was, how the President had said nothing like that would ever happen again, and how foolish I was being.

I moved unhurriedly to the window that faces out over the East River. Nothing unusual was happening. Traffic was passing. People were moving in ordered chaos. A vendor was selling coffee and newspapers at a kiosk across the street. I waited, my heart slamming against my ribs like a frantic bird in a cage, but nothing dragged itself up the muddy banks of the East River. Nothing crawled up onto the suspension wires of the Brooklyn Bridge and began tearing it to shrapnel.

I was being stupid, imagining things, and it was probably the delivery truck rumbling by outside on its Tuesday morning drop, or maybe a news chopper passing overhead. I started breathing again, slowly, in, out, in, out. Anxiety Disorder. Post Traumatic Stress Syndrome. Doctors have all these fancy scientific terms for frantic human terror.

"Kevin?" my dad said from the kitchen. He sounded normal— tired, distracted, but not panicked. Was I imagining everything, I wondered?

Then I glanced down at my hands and finally noticed that my cigarette was on fire. Not burning, mind you, but on fire, the little licking flames inching toward my fingers. "Shit!" I hissed, and threw the cigarette into the toilet and immediately flushed it.

"Kevin!"

"I'm already there!" I called.

Smoking is mondo bad for your health, just FYI.

2

Just my luck, I ran into Mr. Serizawa as I headed out to school. Usually, he stays upstairs in his rooms, which is just fine by me, since he has these crazy Muppet eyes that sort of freak me out.

"*Mago*," he said in greeting, hobbling down the stairs with his carven little cane. "*Mago*, I had a dream about you last night."

You know that crazy Asian dude who gave little Billy the mogwai? Yeah, exactly.

"Hi, Mr. Serizawa," I said.

At least he was speaking English this morning, except for that *Mago* business. It means something casual like son or grandchild. Older Japanese folks use it on young people in a patronizing way that's supposed to make you feel good, but that's about all I'd learned of my dad's native language. Generally speaking, I know less Japanese than the average otaku, which is pretty sad when you think about it.

Mr. Serizawa worked his way down the steps without help. He's not what you'd expect—some wizened old magus in a Kung Fu movie or whatever. He's over eighty years old, and was head chef of various New York bistros most of his life, and a butcher before that, and a soldier before that, if the stories are true. Despite his age, he's built solid like a mountain.

I thought about telling him I had to run, and that I was late for school, but I had a feeling he wouldn't buy it. He's the only one I know who can see right through my fibs—maybe it's the Muppet eyes, I don't know. So I waited impatiently at the bottom of the stairs, my pack over one shoulder, hoping this wouldn't entail some boring long philosophy lesson about a Samurai or something. "What kind of dream did you have, Mr. Serizawa?" I prompted.

He nodded dourly. "You were fighting the Orochi, like the god Susa-no-O," he announced, rolling the words along in a way you just don't hear anymore unless you visit the Japanese countryside where the old dialects are still spoken. "I saw you with a flaming sword, taming the great Kami."

"Oh yeah? Was I saving any girls?"

He laughed. "No girls, but maybe tomorrow night."

I pretended to smile, but what I really wanted to do was to get the hell out of there. I mean, the way Mr. Serizawa studies me has total creepy child molester written all over it. He's never pulled anything, but you can tell he's up to something.

"Did you cut your hair, *Mago*?" he asked, admiring me.

I glanced longingly at the door. "Um…no?"

"Yet something is different this morning. Something has changed."

Yeah, I had taken a shower. Was that it?

"You are older today than you were yesterday," he said. Again he nodded, as if to himself. "Visit me when you are ready, Mago. You will know the time, and I will always be here for you." Turning, he hobbled off to the restaurant's kitchen.

Do you see what I mean about creeeepy?

Rolling my eyes, I ducked out to the converted shed in the alley behind the restaurant before anything weirder could happen—and before my dad could catch me and offer me a lift to school, because I'd never get out of that one. He hates it when I take Jennie out on these streets, and keeps telling me I'm going to break my neck one day. It's a good thing I'm not a gun freak, because then he'd warn me I'm going to shoot my eye out.

Out in the shed, I swung a leg over Jennie's worn and pitted saddle, then stopped a moment just to savor the feel of her under me. The obsolete and totally unfashionable dirt bike was comfortable, waiting for me. As always, it felt like coming home.

As always, I felt a spike of despair once Jennie's engine turned over and snarled to life. It reminded me of Wayne—greasy-fingered Wayne, ponytailed Wayne, Wayne my best (and only) friend, and about how I'd never get a chance to fix an old jalopy like this with him again. Jennie was his magnum opus, named for a girl who wouldn't talk to him at school. Wayne, like so many other things in my life, was gone. He never got a chance to make a total fool of himself by asking Jennie out, and Jennie never got a chance to laugh at him because, she, too, was gone.

3

My second day at Thomas Jefferson High somehow managed to be both uneventful and irritating.

In Algebra, I got a paper back from Mr. Russo, all A-Plussed up with a note attached asking me if I could tutor the "less gifted" students of his class. That made me want to pound my head against the top of my desk until I achieved full unconsciousness. I mean, I wouldn't be caught dead tutoring, even if it does mean meeting a lot of easy and appreciative girls. Michelle sat next to me in Latin, then walked with me to Biology. Mrs. Rodriguez didn't call on me today, so I was able to properly maintain my masquerade as the dumb new guy. By mid-morning, I also learned that the earthquake

I thought I had imagined that morning had been felt by a fair number of other students. In fact, faint tremors had been reported all over the downtown Brooklyn area, according to the closed-circuit KTV broadcast that Mrs. Rodriguez made us watch. That didn't improve my overall opinion of New York much. California is supposed to move around under folks—you kind of expect it—but I'd thought that New York was built on pretty solid bedrock. At one point, during English, the janitor rumbled by the classroom with his bucket and brooms, and the noise made this one uber-nervous girl jump up and run shrieking from the room. I figured that had a lot to do with the colorful rumors going around (probably started by Troy and his meathead friends) that a giant monster was moving under the ground.

That was bad, but what was worse was I didn't see Aimi anywhere in the halls, or in any of the classrooms. I tried not to let that bother me. We didn't share any classes, so it was only natural that we not run into each other until lunch. *Maybe she had gotten sick*, I thought, *or the earthquake had frightened her like the girl in Latin.* Snowman had said she wasn't well, whatever that meant.

The moment I entered the cafeteria, Michelle hanging by my side, my eyes shifted over to find all the kids in black. Aimi wasn't there, though the Goths were amassed in their usual place, doing what they usually did—posing self-importantly and not eating.

Snowman was sitting on the end of the outlaw bench, dressed in a bright green Mad-Hatter-inspired tuxedo and top hat, his bleach-white hair tied back in a long ponytail. I thought he looked like the bastard offspring of Lucky the Leprechaun and Oliver Twist. He was signing a homemade Destroyer album for a girl. The color rushed through the girl's cheeks as he scribbled across the impact case with a silver pen. I rolled my eyes, and when she started jumping up and down like a demented kangaroo, I had to suppress an urge to throw up a little in my mouth.

"I don't get what they see in those clowns," Michelle said while we stood in the lunch line with our trays, waiting to be slopped. She casually reached up and ripped a poster down off the wall advertising the concert at The Hole—Destroyer was playing a double bill with a local girl band I'd never heard of.

I grunted noncommittally and stared down at the free school lunch being dumped on my tray, trying to decide if the mystery substance was made of road kill, or only looked that way, and if I necessarily needed a Hazmat suit in order to consume it.

"And the Willie Wonka clothes...wassup with that?" Michelle made a face.

"Some of it's okay," I said.

"Maybe, but I prefer a guy who looks hot in jeans." She smiled winningly up at me.

I sighed and picked up my tray and followed her to our table, where Terry was busy doing an autopsy on his Netbook, probably so he could upgrade it into a rocket-launcher, à la MacGyver.

I was being hard on Michelle, I knew. She was reliable, down to earth, and normal. The type of girl my dad would dig, but I wasn't sure if I could tolerate her practical, All-American approach to life. All of that wholesome, kinetic energy was likely to give me motion sickness.

For the next half an hour, I pushed the industrial waste that passed for lunch around my tray and tried to pay attention as she chattered on about a bike an uncle of hers had given her. She looked at me pleadingly with her big brown doe eyes. "Could you look at it, Kevin? Please? I think I'm going to make it my Shop project, but I was hoping you could help me with the alignment. My dad is always working, so I can't ask him."

"You have a bike?" I said. I stopped Goth-watching and turned my full attention on Michelle. It wasn't like Aimi was going to appear mystically in the middle of the cafeteria just to make me feel better.

Michelle's face lit up. "It's a VTX Interceptor. V-4 engine, but my dad is helping me to upgrade it."

"You're kidding," I said. "The new Hondas? Those are killer."

Michelle nodded, secure in the knowledge that she finally had me. "My uncle races them up in the Pocono raceways." She gave me a close-lipped smile, her face flushing as she suddenly turned shy, and picked daintily at the salad she had chosen over the Road Kill Du Jour entre that I was trying not to gag over. I wondered if I had anything to do with that. "But he trashed this one. I mean, it's a great cruiser, but he can't maneuver on the track with it anymore, so he gave it to me as an early graduation present."

Wow, a family who gave each other retired, top-of-the-line bikes. Why did I have to be born into a family whose one ambition in life was to make the perfect rice ball? I mean, does my karma suck or what?

"Kevin, I saw your bike, man, it's awesome!" Terry surfaced long enough to proclaim. "Can I take it for a ride sometime?"

"Terry," Michelle said with exasperation, "you wouldn't fit on Kevin's bike."

"I will after I make the football team," Terry insisted.

"Troy and his fathead friends will slaughter you," Michelle countered, looking appalled.

"Shows what you know, Shell. Wait till I make a touchdown. And then..." And here Terry got up to do a bizarre end-zone dance, even as Michelle bit her plastic fork and rolled her eyes at me as if to say, *As if that's ever going to happen.*

I tried not to smile, but Terry's victory dance was pretty funny—I had to give him props for his I-don't-give-a-damn-who's-looking attitude. "I love that bike," he babbled, sitting down again at the table. "Doesn't John Woo use those in all this films?"

"I'm not sure," I said, "maybe, but it sort of needs work."

All at once, bikes were the topic. Michelle said her dad did custom paint jobs at his garage in the Heights, and she had access to just about every kind of tool or paint I might need to upgrade Jennie—which, for me, was pretty much like turning a starving kid loose in a candy shop. Terry said he knew "carputers" and could hack anything with wires. I got so into what they were saying, I stopped thinking about Aimi for a whole half an hour.

4

The rest of my week was positively sucktastic—especially at the end, when the monster tried to eat me.

In Computer Lab, I got a partner who turned out to be the only kid left on planet Earth who didn't know how to use a PC, except to download porn. P.E. was only minimally better—I didn't have a uniform yet, so Coach Kuznik let me sit it out on the bleachers instead of wrestling down on the mat and making a fool of myself.

In Biology, Mrs. Rodriguez said we were going to be studying Karkadon's anatomy in detail, and I almost walked out after that announcement.

Friday afternoon, seconds after the last bell rang, found me standing beside Jennie in the parking lot, pulling my riding gloves on and watching all the other students scurrying en masse toward their vehicles. The skate guys set up their ramp, and the pusher guys were back at the fence. I watched the Goths climb aboard their black van, minus Aimi.

For the fourth day in a row, Aimi had failed to show for school. It had taken a lot of subtle digging on my part, but I had managed to get at least some information out of Michelle, who disliked Aimi even more than she did Snowman, which was saying a lot. According to the stories, Aimi was suffering from a mystery illness and her attendance in school was sporadic, at best. Aimi never talked about it, but the rumors ran from an incurable childhood disease like leukemia or Multiple Sclerosis, to various STDs. Michelle was leaning toward the STDs, even though I was having a hard time believing that. Aimi just didn't seem the type, somehow.

I wondered if she would be at the concert on Saturday. I wondered if she was well enough to play. I thought about asking Snowman if she was okay, but I was pretty sure he would just punch me in the face. I was fingering the note in my pocket I had been carrying around with me all week like a magic talisman, thinking about what to do, when I saw Terry waving enthusiastically to me.

I waved back, just to be nice. That's me, Mr. Nice Guy.

Terry, being Terry, misinterpreted it and bounded over, his fat jiggling girlishly under his Darth Maul T-shirt and outdated patch jacket. "Sweeeet ride, man," he said, staring wild-eyed at Jennie and doing that victory dance of his in a totally embarrassing way.

"Thanks, man," I said, glancing around to see if anyone was noticing us together. I mean, I felt for the guy—obviously, he was in need of a cool card, but I didn't have any extras to lend him. I turned the engine over, hoping he'd get a clue and go catch his bus.

No dice. Terry was still looking my bike over like she was completely edible. "She have a killswitch? 'Cause I can rewire that for you, man."

I weighed hanging with Terry versus a bike that wouldn't die if I hit too high an MPH. Without the killswitch, I could go fast enough to alter time, but then, Terry would be a permanent fixture in my life, and Terry was no Wayne. Gah. It was like a conundrum of epic proportions.

"You can do that?" I finally said. Yeah, I could hardly believe I had just said that.

Terry grinned and his eyes lit up like Christmas lights behind his glasses. "No problem, man. Terry-saurus Rex can hack it. Didn'ja notice there's no locks on the school computers? I have the whole place wired, man. Hack city." I had noticed that, actually, considering the amount of porn my lab partner was able to download. Terry folded his arms old school Vanilla Ice style, trying waaay too hard to earn that cool card, as far as I was concerned. "Tell me I'm the man."

As I watched the black van pull out of the parking lot, inspiration hit me, a way to find out what I needed to know about Aimi without going to Snowman. I turned my attention back on Terry. "Rex," I said, "you are the man. If I ever need to get inside the Pentagon computer, you'll be my go-to guy."

He developed a sly look. "Rex," he said with approval. "That rocks, man." He smiled like he could probably do it, too.

5

Technically speaking, I don't have a curfew. My dad's a pretty straight guy. He trusts me to be home before nightfall, unless something's come up, in which case, I'm supposed to phone. So by visiting The Hole and not telling him, I was breaking the unwritten rules. The concert was from seven to nine, and my dad never wanders up to the loft before nine anyway, so I figured I could catch the concert and still make it home before him if I left a little earlier than everyone else.

In my defense, I hadn't expected all hell to break loose. I swear. More on that later.

The Hole looked pretty seedy from the outside, the kind of place where drug dealers in action movies hired professional assassins to knock off the competition. Needless to say, my dad would have had a triple cow if he saw it. As I rode toward the building, I stared up at the age-pitted brownstone, grey and almost luminous in the dim street lights, with black iron bars over the windows and an iron gate in front of the door.

I parked Jennie around back, in the weedy little lot adjacent to the chain link-fenced backyard of the project next door. There seemed to be a lot of cars, but just to be sure, I walked around the corner and found the colorful murals of graffiti emblazoned on the side of the building that I'd heard about. The place looked like a condemnable dive, but it was definitely it.

The heavy pneumatic door had the words ABANDON HOPE ALL YE WHO ENTER spray-painted across it—not an encouraging sight. I stopped and stared at it, wondering what I hoped to gain from this little venture. I mean, Snowman hadn't been kidding when he'd said Aimi had problems.

Terry's hacked school computers had inspired me earlier. I'm not exactly a cyber-slacker, after all. After making it home from school, I sat down at my dinosaur of a laptop and did some serious web research.

It wasn't difficult to find Destroyer information and fan blogs on Facebook, Tumblr, all the usual suspects. True to what Michelle had said, Aimi's fans considered her a "bad girl," the kind of girl that all the guys wanted, but wouldn't dare bring home to meet their families. She had been expelled from virtually every school in New York City. Rumor had it that she'd spent more time in rehabilitation clinics for various addictions than River Phoenix, had at least two DUIs on her record, and had been a cutter since she was thirteen years old. She had a social worker and a therapist, neither of which seemed to be doing her any good.

Her dad was loaded, so, as you can imagine, that helped a lot. He was used to getting Aimi out of all kinds of fixes with plenty of money and maybe a few threats on the side. *Maybe*, I thought, *Aimi really was sick.* So sick, she was living for everything it was worth, trying to cram a lifetime into a few short years of life. She wouldn't be the first. Some of the kids who'd survived San

Francisco had turned kamikaze, like they had to prove again and again that they were really, truly alive. Some wound up in the news for alcohol or drug-related crimes. Some went to prison, and more than a few had landed in mental health institutions.

As I'd read various blogs, I'd felt a sick knot tighten in my stomach at the thought that Aimi was on the short road to self-implosion. I had no idea how I could help her, but I knew I needed to talk to her. I had to know she was all right. I steeled myself, grabbed the door handle, and pulled. Then I was in.

The club was low and almost pitch black under the dimly burning blacklights. I saw a rundown juice bar, a dozen tables scattered around, and a raised stage that dominated most of the floor. Pop star watercolor murals, foreign movie posters, and fliers for various local bands covered the otherwise derelict walls.

A group of kids in glittery dark club wear floated by, making me feel direly underdressed in my jeans and jacket. I was about to follow them when the doorman asked to see my ID. I flashed him my driver's license, and when he saw it, he said I shouldn't worry about the cover charge. I wondered if Aimi had had anything to do with that, or if I just looked so damned destitute that he felt sorry for me. He stamped my hand, and then I was swallowed into the dimness and thudding heartbeat of The Hole. Vendors lurked in the shadows, selling overpriced T-shirts, music CDs, and cheap homemade jewelry. I tasted cloves and saw wisps of smoke rising as thick as cream through the blue and red strobe lights.

I'd been half-thinking about the crushed pack of extra-light Newports in my jeans pocket all day. I'm not proud of the habit, mind you, but if you want to talk health with me, you ought to know I inhaled enough tar and debris in San Francisco to pave a road twice over. I'll be a lucky to see fifty without being on an oxygen tank. A Newport now and again isn't likely to have a huge impact on all the fun future health issues I knew I was sure to face. After that little incident with the flaming cigarette, I'd been reluctant to light up. Nobody told me that cigarettes were combustible.

Onstage, twin girls in vinyl silver cyber dresses and flight goggles were screaming hoarsely into the mike, and stomping their monster plats rhythmically against the stage. Everyone was on the dance floor, back dancing frantically in and out of the motion-detection lights, but I wasn't going anywhere near the dance floor, thanks, but I'm not that brave. Instead, I installed myself in a dark corner table and waited.

Around eight, the owner climbed up on the stage to introduce the band. Around that time, they started taking donations. The bartender came around, asking if I wanted to donate to the San Francisco Relief & Rebuilding Fund. I felt like saying, *What San Francisco?* But like everyone else, I dug dutifully through my wallet and spotted the guy a fiver, even though that meant no smokes for me for the rest of the week.

All the kids in the club—the place was more mobbed than ever—migrated to the front of the stage to mull and weave in anticipation. Then the band appeared from backstage and started climbing up to the stage, hefting their heavy instruments with them, and everyone started whooping and stomping. I stayed where I was, back in the shadows, and just watched.

I spotted Aimi lugging an enormous cello case onstage and felt my heart lift a little. She was dressed in a huge black birthday dress of a gown that looked like something from Revolutionary France, froths of lace and bows everywhere. Her face was a death mask of white, with blue and black henna scrawled around her eyes in crazy loops. She looked so small and doll-like up there, like the crowd could swallow her alive. Yet, she handled the cello with surprising strength and dexterity, uncasing it, bending it to her bow.

Snowman, dressed in an outrageous suit of black glitter and reams of white ruffles, like a Gothic version of Liberace, moved to the microphone up front. The audience (mostly girls) cheered and catcalled shamelessly. He gave them a cocky smile and slung an electric guitar around his broad shoulders. The other members of the band took up their instruments and began several slow strains of music. Snowman cupped the mike in his hands, eyed the audience in a serpentine way, and said low and sly into it: "This...is a restoration..."

The Indian girl who looked like Raggedy Anne launched in first with the violin, playing it like a gypsy. Aimi followed with the cello, and the African-American twins filled in with keyboard and drums. I was expecting boring "big" orchestra music, but it was loud, raucous, and it pretty much rocked.

Snowman began thrashing side-to-side in rhythm, rapping harshly over the beat, whipping the audience into a frenzy and pounding a shiver down my spine with his snarling, throat-tearing lyrics:

Yeah! This is a restoration
What can't you understand? You can't key my plan
Oh yeah! This is my respiration
Don't touch me don't touch the plan don't touch the man who
plants the seed

I learned a grudging respect for Snowman in that moment. He was an ass—but a talented ass. He had a voice like a throttled chainsaw. He knew his guitar, could tear riffs from it like a demonic version of Eddie Van Halen. Not to mention he had this thing—he started charging back and forth across the stage, singing directly at the audience like he meant every word of the message for them. Nothing hesitant, nothing afraid. Like he owned the stage. Like he owned the world.

Hell. Don't think about who it is, man, I thought, *just enjoy the music.*

But that was just it. I was.

And it was pissing me off.

6

Kids mobbed the stage the minute the band had finished their third encore. There was no way I was getting through that solid, impenetrable wall of sweating taffeta and brocade. Feeling somewhat letdown since there was no way I was going to see Aimi tonight, I decided to give it up.

Trying not to look like a lovesick puppy that had been kicked, I started for the door. As I was stepping outside, the doorman handed me a sheet of paper (I noticed immediately that it was the same material as the letter) and a little wink.

It said:

Meet me out back. I've missed you. —Aimi

7

I sat side-saddle on the bike behind the club, a wormy nervousness crawling down my spine, listening to the sounds of cabs blaring in the street as they moved uptown, and the occasional, jarring whine of a siren. I kept looking at Aimi's note, trying to decide if it was for real. Maybe it was a joke. A really cruel joke Aimi was playing me. In a minute or so, she'd step outside with the band and they'd all point and laugh at the idiot new boy sitting here, waiting for her. There was no other reasonable explanation.

Just then, the back door opened and I saw Aimi standing on the stoop of the club in her big black birthday dress. She lifted her skirts and descending the steps to the pavement, looking like a negative version of Scarlett O'Hara racing breathlessly down the stairwell on her way to meeting Rhett Butler. I sat up and looked around, but I didn't spot Snowman anywhere. She seemed to be alone.

"Kevin," she said, coming to a stop inches from me. She let the hem of her dress drop. "You came to the show!"

I crumpled up the note and hid it in my pocket. I had been thinking about what I would say to her all night, but now that it came down to it, the only thing I could think of was, "Yeah. The show. I came." I sounded so lame, mostly because I was. I was finally going to be able to talk to Aimi alone, and I had no idea what to say. On top of it, I was feeling pretty horrible about the ugly thoughts I'd had about her.

She bit her lip. Her makeup was perfect, doll-like, and her expression expectant, like she was waiting for me to say something. "I liked it," I added, trying not to sound like a complete moron. "It was a really good show."

Her dark eyes flickered up, down. She was as stoic and austere as a character in an Emily Bronte novel. I was afraid I had blown it with just about the most perfect girl in the whole world, when she finally smiled, and her whole face lit up. "Good," she said. "I was so nervous...with you in the audience, I mean. Watching and everything. I almost missed my cue!"

"You were nervous?" Somehow, I couldn't believe that—that I could inspire anyone else to nervousness. It didn't seem even remotely possible. "You were so good! I never noticed."

We both laughed at the ridiculousness of the situation, and the ice was broken. I knew then it would be okay between us. She came and sat down on the bike with me. "Of course I was nervous! You're just about the biggest hottie in school—well, you and Snowman—but everyone is too afraid to talk to you. Haven't you noticed all the girls in the halls always watching you?"

I shook my head to show her I had no idea what she was talking about. What girls? What watching?

She gave me a solemn look and put her hand out, actually touching my arm. I would never wash that arm again, I swear. "There aren't that many people here who are like us...different, I mean. Not at school, anyway," she said. "Do you ever get teased about being different, Kevin?"

I licked my wind-chapped lips, searching for the right words. "Well...sure," I said, my voice choking up a little because I could smell her chocolaty perfume and it was making me feel dizzy. I just kept staring at her, probably solidifying her opinion of me as a total idiot. She was so adorable, so yummy, I couldn't imagine anyone teasing her about anything, especially not anything so pathetic as being half Japanese. "I always figure, if someone is stupid enough just to look at the differences and nothing else, and that bothers them, then that's not someone I want to hang with."

Her eyes grew as large and grave as space. "I never thought of it that way. I usually just get mad. Then things happen. Then my dad gets mad at me for losing control, then it all gets worse, you know?"

I nodded, thinking about what I had read, all the schools she had been thrown out of, wondering if that was it, and what it must have been like for her. "There are times when I wish I had gotten mad, but I never did, not till...not till I moved here." I almost said not till my mom died, but I decided I didn't want to go there. Aimi didn't need to shovel my emotional crap.

Aimi bit her lip in sympathy. "Things must be really different here than they were in San Francisco. It must be like another planet."

I shrugged. Yes, no, maybe. "A little," I said, but I didn't want to talk about San Francisco. That was like another planet, one that didn't exist anymore. "You play a wicked cello," I said to change the subject. "I mean, I never thought of it as a 'cool' instrument, not until tonight."

She smiled a smile that could have lit up all of downtown Brooklyn. "Snowman taught me. He can play seven instruments," she said, glancing fondly over at the club. Then she read something in my face—I guess I was pretty transparent about my opinion of Snowman—because she added, "I'm not dating him, just so you know. Snowman is Snowman. He's...well, he's different too. He's like a big brother to me. The brother I wish I'd had."

She had been going to say something else. What, I didn't know, but like me, she had changed her mind mid-sentence. I just wondered what that other thing was. "In the beginning, it was just the two of us, playing guitar," she said, glancing off into the night. "Then the others joined. Morta. Dust and Ashes."

The twins were named Dust and Ashes? I mean, were they serious?

Aimi dropped her eyes, lashes like fallen soot on her porcelain cheeks. "I know you think it's silly. That we're silly. All of us. Maybe we are. Maybe nothing will ever come of the band, but Snowman's music helped me. He helped me through so many bad times, Kevin. You have no idea."

"He said you two were best friends."

I didn't want to actually say it, but there is was, lying between us like the great big gothic elephant in the room. I waited for her to look up, to tell me that was none of my business, but she only looked sad and a little defeated. "He is my best friend. He tutors me when I'm too sick to come to school. He's always been there for me, even when my dad wasn't." She looked up with an expression of profound pain. "Oh, Kevin, there's so much you don't know. So much you don't understand about me. So much out there that's bigger than us."

I didn't know what to say, what was appropriate, so I just took her thin little lacy hand in mine. She looked up at that, surprised by that simple contact, which broke my heart. She looked so fragile, so small, in the big black dress. I just wanted to take her, hold her, and take away all the pain and loneliness she had undoubtedly dealt with for years.

Honestly, I wanted to kiss her in that moment, more than I had ever wanted to kiss anyone. I think she knew, because she tilted her face up and said, "*Chuushite kudasai,*" with a small, playful smile. "That means…"

"I know what it means, and I know that it's polite in Japanese culture to always ask." I'd been hitting the language books, you see. "Um…*chuushite kudasai?*"

"*Hai,*" she answered.

I moved my hand up to her hair and touched it softly. It felt as soft as the fur of a kitten. I wondered if her solemn white face would feel just as soft. I touched it and was surprised by her coolness. I traced the contour of her cheek and the shape of her lips. She closed her eyes and laughed nervously. "Your hands are very warm, Kevin," she said. "That doesn't mean you have a cold heart, does it?"

I glanced down and wondered if I was seeing things correctly—my hands seemed to be glowing with a faint golden light. *It has to be the poor neon lighting here*, I thought. There was no other explanation. I dropped my hands to Aimi's shoulders and drew her gently to me. We leaned in close and she tilted her head. My world was filled with her scrumptious perfume in the seconds before Snowman suddenly appeared right beside us.

I swear I never saw him coming. He just materialized out of nowhere. I thought for sure he would push me, the way he had at school, but I guess he'd had enough. This time, he executed a right hook that impressed the hell out of me even as I went down hard on the gravel. I didn't feel a thing—that would come later, after the adrenaline rush had worn off.

I sat up immediately.

Snowman's tall, sweating, and shaking form loomed high over me, both fists clenched. I noticed with some perverse joy that he had broken knuckles and was bleeding all over his fancy outfit. "Told you, hothead," he warned, "Leave. Aimi. Alone."

I tasted the blood of my broken lip. "Yeah, well," I said as calmly as possible, "fuck you, chief." I climbed slowly to my feet, swaying slightly. He was standing between me and Aimi, so I got up against him. "Get out of my way, Snow White."

"Make me."

"Stop it!" Aimi screamed at us both. "Just stop it!"

He punched me again.

He was good. I went down hard on my hands and knees, a buzz of pain in my head. The parking lot shifted slightly, like the world was on a giant cosmic pendulum. I heard voices. The rest of the band was gathering around our private little Fight Club, some of them yelling at Snowman to cut it out, that he was acting like a jerk, others edging him on. I ignored them. They didn't exist. Only Snowman existed. I spit a penny-sized droplet of blood onto the pavement and began climbing slowly to my feet again.

"Just stay down!" Snowman yelled.

I got up, instead.

He tried to kick me in the ribs with his monster plats, but I moved too fast. I wasn't that chubby kid who played video games and read books all day. Not anymore. I threw myself against him, grabbed him by the cravat, and together we crashed back against the chain-link fence behind us. Snowman grunted as he took the full force of the impact. I was going to say something smarmy before busting his teeth in, but something brushed the back of my neck, distracting me. At first, I thought it must be a fly, then I realized the hairs on the back of my neck were standing at full, rigid attention. My skin was crawling like it was on fire…

A moment later, I found out why.

Because a moment later, the street exploded behind us, and a kaiju rose screaming like a thing from hell above the inferno.

CHAPTER THREE
Break Stuff

1

The explosion that heralded the end of my life and the beginning of my nightmare rocked the entire street from side to side. All of us went down, clutching the pavement, as dozens of car alarms went off, adding to the rising cacophony in the night. Something told me we were in trouble—the type of trouble that would cost us our lives if we didn't keep our heads together. I sat up, gritting my teeth with determination, and scrambled backward. I didn't stop until I hit the fence.

Something had happened, something that was going to change the world. Again.

The street was full of smoke and the raw smell of sewage. Ironically, the first thing I thought of was not that some creature was responsible for that, but that a gas main had exploded on the avenue, or a bomb had gone off. This was New York. Crime happened in New York. Terrorists set fire to buildings.

Then the street rattled grittily and cracks spider-crawled across the pocked asphalt. It reminded me of the earthquake I had felt several days ago, taken to the tenth power. The street rolled and several cabs flipped over like toys. I was afraid, finally, down in my bones, where the basest survival instincts lurk.

I crawled unsteadily to my feet, covered in grit and blood and freezing sweat, and turned to look at Aimi and Snowman clinging to the fence for support. My mind was clear and alert and painfully sober. The first thing I did was grab Snowman by the front of his fancy glitter jacket and push him stumbling toward Aimi. "Get her out of here," I said. "Get them all out of here, now!"

He blinked at me, clearly shaken, our conflict forgotten for the moment. Then he nodded, and turned to assist Aimi, and then the rest of the band, over the fence.

I didn't stay to watch. Behind me, beyond veils of smoke, came the worst sound imaginable, a screaming the likes of which you would expect to hear emerging from the bowels of hell. I stepped out into the street, looking at the people lying in the gutters like broken dolls. The explosion had brought traffic to a screeching halt, and cars were jam-packed every which way on the avenue like a kid's toy collection.

The street trembled again, and again I heard that noise: like someone running a metal glove over a blackboard.

I walked out into the street, feeling like the token Asian in a spaghetti western about to go out and face the gunfighter villain. I thought of sirens, fires, ineffectual police squads firing on the monster that crawled out of San Francisco Bay two years ago. I walked, but I walked afraid. I knew I had to buy Aimi and Snowman time to get away, but my throat was dry and clicked when I tried to swallow. All around me people were struggling to escape their cars, banging doors against the vehicles packed against them, breaking windshields, crawling through jagged glass with no hesitation for fear or pain as their own basic instincts for survival kicked in. Ragged people in ragged clothes and blood...

The earthquake, I thought. *Something huge was moving under the street. And now that* something *was here...*

An injured businessman staggered into the street. Maybe he was trying to help, or maybe he was only in a state of shock, but he reached a car with a family trapped inside it and tried yanking open the passenger-side door, which only banged against the side of the idling cabbie that had slammed into it at the intersection.

I didn't think. I pushed him aside. The family in the car was screaming. I slid the jacket off my shoulders, wrapped my forearm in the thick material, and bashed in the passenger-side window with my fist. "Get out!" I shouted. "Get out of here now!"

As they began scrambling out, I moved to the center of the street. Surrounded by the massive pile-up, I stared at the belching smoke coming from a half dozen open manholes. Something was out there, in the smoke and darkness, something I couldn't see...yet.

Smoke closed in around me, obscuring my vision and making greasy halos of the light on the avenue. The man I had been trying to help began to scream, to scream the way a man should never scream.

It's like that night, I thought. *The night the thing crawled out of the sea and began trampling the people as they tried desperately to get away. The nightmare is starting all over again...*

A black thing writhed in the smoke. It stank of sewage, well-rotted fish, ozone, nightmare. The stink of it was in my nose and in my hair, and I knew it would be days before I was rid of it. If I lived that long.

Suddenly, manhole covers popped all up and down the street and black, snakelike tentacles began wriggling along the ground. There must have been a dozen of them. I tried to figure out what it was, the vile black thing swaying darkly in the mist. Centipede, snake, eel, caterpillar. It was all of those, none of those. I felt my heart and bowels fall as the thing quivered into view only a few feet from me, a pulsating black mass that became more apparent as the smoke cleared. It was twenty feet high and as thick around as an old oak tree. I could see no head, no face, just a wall of darkness raining down putrid, black, oily water on the street. I heard a dull thudding noise that seemed to emanate from the very earth itself. It took me several moments to recognize it as a heartbeat so powerful the ground itself carried a wild current.

The earthquake...it suddenly made a lot more sense.

The thing curled over like a curious foraging centipede, the tip expanding into a bulbous, pod-like head. I stayed frozen in place, but the businessman in the street started screaming hysterically. Something unzipped itself across the thing's face, a vertical insect jaw lined with jagged teeth that drooled clear mucus. I saw the jaws on the Venus flytrap head flex, once. Then the monster emitted a cackling bellow that sounded both amused and victorious at the same time, and it shot downward, swallowing the man whole, in mid-scream. It emitted a terrible clicking noise as it swallowed, then began searching for more prey.

I thought about screaming myself. It seemed like a really good idea at that moment, but something paralyzed me. All I could do was stand there and watch, wide-eyed, electric with fright, as the thing swayed overhead, searching for more prey. It wouldn't take long before it detected me, I knew. I clenched my hands, noticing that they felt hot, like two irons in the fire.

I glanced down, and despite the craziness of the situation, it actually got crazier in that moment—because I finally realized that my hands were on fire.

2

Gaping, I wondered what I had done to deserve this hell. I mean, I'm not a bad kid. Really. I don't cut class, smoke crack, backtalk teachers, or set bugs on fire with magnifying glasses. I'm a really dull person. I think karma was picking on the wrong guy tonight.

Yet, despite it all, I wasn't really afraid, either. Unclenching my hands, I realized the flames were blue and almost cold to the touch. They leaped up, a column of fire within, which I recognized a familiar object—one of those things you recognize even if you've never seen one up close and personal. It was insane, completely unlikely...but I know a samurai sword when I see one. I immediately gripped the hilt. I knew if I could just hold the sword, I wouldn't be afraid of the monster anymore. Hey, it worked for Saint George.

The monster's mouth clicked open. I felt a spattering of hot saliva on my cheeks.

I was afraid, and yet, I was not afraid.

Naturally, I thought of Mr. Serizawa. *You were fighting the Orochi, like Susa-no-O.*

What a stupid, cheesy name, I thought even as the monster suddenly snapped at me with its wide, jagged-toothed jaws.

I expected to be dead. Chomped. My hand had moved faster than my eye, faster than it had ever moved before. Suddenly, the sword that was on fire—or rather, the sword that was made of fire—had cut through the spongy flesh and left the "head" flopping around on the ground like a giant black fish out of water.

The ground shook as the creature, much larger than I had expected, screamed in agony beneath me. Black fluid spurted from the truncated appendage as it flailed, smashing wetly into the street, covering everything in a burning black slime that immediately ate through the asphalt like the most caustic acid, and where it touched abandoned cars, ate them right down to their axels. The street rocked, and windows chattered apart on the upper floors of buildings on both sides of the street. Finally, the monstrous thing began sinking back down the hole into the ground. To the earth. To the water. Back to the unknown depths from which it had come. The other shrieking, swaying pod-headed appendages immediately followed suit, disappearing one after another.

It was gone in seconds, as if it had never been, but it left behind a path of broken cars, bodies, and glassy destruction that littered the street up and down. I was about to let out my breath in relief when the whole street heaved upward and cracked open.

Like a rancid asphalt egg, it birthed a new kaiju into the world.

3

There are things you never forget, things stamped down deep into your memory, like footprints in wet sand. The day you fell from a tree and broke your arm. The day you made a fool of yourself in front of a girl you liked. The first time you really fell in love…and the first time you realized the monster was about to get you.

The sound the kaiju made as it surfaced is something I'll ever forget. Claws on blackboard, child screaming, women weeping, knife singing as it sinks deep into your gut. It sounded like all these things. The appendages I had seen were only a small part of the whole beast, I realized. The monster that ploughed out of the massive hole in the street looked like a fish, or frog, or something no one had ever heard of before.

I scrambled out of the way, amazed at how analytical I could be, considering it was easily the size of a house, and as black as pitch and shining with wet, razor-sharp scales. Its humped back was covered in those snakelike appendages with the Venus flytrap heads, making it look like something out of old H. P. Lovecraft's worst nightmare. It stank of sewage and death, and the smell of it made me want to gag.

I didn't. I was too fascinated by the sight of the thing's grotesque, barely-formed head, the reddish, heavily lidded, almost human-like eyes glaring at me with a cunning and evil intelligence. I stood there, outside the club, listening to a series of popping explosions as the beast tore up various gas mains in its wriggling effort to emerge.

It finally settled atop the street like a mountain of burning black slime, making that sound again, like it was laughing at me, laughing at the sheer puniness of mankind. I should have been afraid of it. Instead, I swung the burning sword around two-handedly, ready to take another piece out of it. Under the circumstances, there wasn't much else I could do.

It eyed me cautiously.

"Afraid?" I said, then kicked myself mentally when it dawned on me that agitating a monster was a lot different than doing it to a bully. Bullies didn't normally try to eat you.

It hissed at me and leaped into the sky. For a moment, the lights of the city were eclipsed as it passed overhead. Then it crashed down atop the roof of the club across the street. The structure exploded under the monster's weight like it was made of tinker toys. I staggered back as dust and debris spilled all the way out into the street and surrounded me. I could hardly believe it had moved so fast…or that the whole building lay crushed beneath it in seconds, with everyone still inside.

The street looked like a demolition zone, surreal, like the end of the world in some post apocalyptic movie. The only thing missing were the zombies. The creature made that hissing/cackling noise like it was pleased with itself and its work.

I stared at the overturned cars, the broken bodies, the bloodied glass scattered everywhere. The wind sighed, blowing the yellowish debris around as if we stood on a devastated planet, the victim of a cataclysmic nuclear war. A poster blew against me, then blew away. I coughed as the dust began to clear. I finally saw a girl lying in the rubble at my feet, her fancy club wear ripped to bloody tatters on her still body. Ignoring the monster, I knelt down, pushing aside the debris atop her and checked for a pulse, but she was as lifeless as a mannequin.

I wiped the soot off her face. She was my age. Pretty. She was one of the girls who had been giggling about me in the halls of my high school.

My mind went calm, my horror far away, but my anger burned. It burned like the sword I still gripped in my hands.

I stood up. I swung the sword high overhead, not because I thought I could actually destroy the monster with my puny little weapon, but because I was following a predetermined pattern, carving a complex symbol into the aim before me, even though I had no idea what I was doing. But my hands knew, even if my brain was too numb to understand what was happening.

Two signs. Japanese characters. Kanji. They seemed to take on a glow in the very air before me. I knew what they meant. I knew what they summoned. I knew from the dream. I had seen the same characters burned into the book.

What am I doing? I wondered, but somehow, I knew. I raised the burning sword in a salute to the night sky painted with a billion ancient stars, and I thought, for no apparent reason at all, *Come.* Then I swung it around so the blade was pointed toward the ground and I drove the blade into the asphalt between my feet with all of my strength. Logic stated that the blade should have broken on contact, but this was obviously no ordinary sword. The sword and the ground were now fused, as if they had always been one. I held the hilt, feeling the vibration of the impact all the way up to my aching shoulders.

Come, I thought, as the wind picked up around me, spilling my hair all over my face. The night was full of the stink of blood and fire. "Come!" I screamed. "Come now!"

The asphalt under my feet split as a fork of lightning struck the sword, making me blink and shudder. I felt a wave of heat so intense it made my skin tighten and crawl. The spit in my mouth dried up and my hands felt like they were burning. With a cry, I released the hilt of the sword and stumbled back.

A column of flame burst from the crack I had made in the street, growing larger by the moment, until it was a full-fledge bonfire so tall it could lick at a ten-story building. I fell back in the gutter, shielding my face from the intense, scalding heat, and watched the air shimmer around me like it was coming off a desert deadpan. Something within the flames roared. It sounded like a train when you're so close to the tracks you can feel the noise vibrating in your bones. Above, the stars seemed to go out and blood red veins of forked lightning snaked outward across a pitch-black sky, followed by an answering roar of thunder. A storm without rain, I thought. It felt like I had been transported to some remote bowel of hell.

Maybe I'm dreaming all this, I thought. Or maybe I was as crazy. There was no other reasonable explanation.

I had thought nothing stranger could happen this night, but it turned out the thing that sounded like a derailed train was taking form in the flames. I hissed between my teeth at the deathless brilliance of it. I decided that the old artists who painted wall scrolls and shoji screens that adorned so many traditional Japanese homes really had no idea what they were doing when they depicted the holy Kami—the gods of ancient Japan. They had never seen one with their own eyes, and that was for sure. They based their artwork on something earthly, tangible, something that could be understood with human eyes and grasped by a human brain. A dragon, tiger, or crane type of thing. This went beyond all that.

This was made of nightmare fabric. As it came into clear focus, I saw scales and fur and feathers all at once, at every point of its body, something at once like a lion but also like an armored dragon, with a face both bestial and strangely human, and a massive head crowned with a myriad of curling horns that extended all the way down its back and the long line of its serpentine tail. All of it was on fire, crackling with the power of a sun gone supernova. It set its giant, iron-clawed feet on the ground before me and flicked its tail, a wall of sulfuric heat so intense it was like standing before a blast furnace. *The eyes*, I thought, raising my arms to shield my face from the intense, baking heat. *The eyes are human...the eyes are blue.*

It growled softly, a sound that slowly escalated into that train-wreck noise I had heard earlier, a noise that ripped up and down my spine. As it tipped its horned head to the heavens and let loose with the full strength of its scorching voice, I dropped to my knees in front of the sword still wedged in the ground, my hands over my ears, trembling body and soul, completely overwrought by the sight of it.

Master, a sexless voice said clearly into my ear, though no one stood there. *You called. I came. What do you desire?*

My head felt like it had nails being pounded into it with every syllable. "Who…who the fuck are you?" I screamed.

It eyed me keenly, like a great cat, then let loose another roar so loud it sandpapered my face and left my ears ringing long afterward. To me, the roar sounded like a name. Like *Raiju*.

Again came the voice in my head, belching and angry: *I lose patience, little boy. What do you desire? Why do you summon the greatest of the ancient Kami?*

I nearly crumbled at the sound of it. I turned to the first monster that I had nearly forgotten existed. It was undulating in the street, eyeing the larger newcomer with a rolling, wild-eyed fright. I thought of the dead girl in the debris. I thought, obliquely, *Kill this creature that has killed these children. Destroy it utterly.*

Raiju laughed, the sound purring through my brain. *I like you, Master*, it said, *we shall certainly be friends.* Then it turned and leaped with feline grace at the first monster.

The frog-thing attempted to retreat, but Raiju's sword-sized claws flashed out as it plowed remorselessly into it. The impact drove both beasts back into a line of brownstone projects, crushing them as if they were made of plastic. I shuddered at the sight of Raiju savagely ripping long, flaming wounds in the monster's black hide. Then the two kaiju started rolling over and over in the debris, kicking up sparks from the buildings and ripping loose bits of unnatural flesh from each other as they went at it literally tooth and nail.

Blood and debris rained down around me, smelling of ozone and red death. The sounds the beasts made were like machines on full power, clanking and grinding together.

What have I done? I thought. *Oh, what have I done?*

And how do I undo it?

Raiju reared up and managed to flip the smaller monster onto its back, its tender underbelly exposed to the flashing black claws, but the first monster was more resourceful than it looked. It opened its massive, froglike mouth, and its tongue—long, slick-black and barbed like a deadly weapon—darted out and smashed into Raiju's flaming shoulder. The tongue stuck solidly in the gold-plated flesh like a projectile weapon.

Raiju reared back, bits of flame raining down over the street like weird, otherworldly snow, but the barbs held. The black beast let out its chuckling chalkboard laugh, as a number of snake-like appendages whipped out and encircled Raiju's neck and legs, biting fiercely down. Now, with its opponent well in hand, it reached up and scratched at the massive, lion-like face with its flippery claws. Raiju roared in anguish, baring dagger-like teeth to the heavens while fire from its shorn mane drifted down to alight the remnants of the projects. It swung its claws at the barbed tongue stuck in its shoulder, the black flesh ripping like hemp with a snapping noise. Finally, it swiped at the other appendages, each of them bursting like rotted vines and falling to the street below, where they cooled into lines of black ash.

Defeated, bleeding and wounded, the first monster somersaulted over its opponent, righting itself on the flaming tarmac before retreating a step.

Raiju rubbed at its face with its forepaw in a gesture almost human, then shook itself and stood up again, towering at least forty stories over the sticklike remnants of the row houses and establishments it was crushing into debris. It let out an earth-rattling roar I was certain could be heard as far south as the Long Island Sound.

I was sweating from pain and electric with fear, but I was too numbed by the sight of the battle before me even to react.

Raiju lunged forward, clacking its massive, catlike jaws at its opponent in warning. The black, froglike beast hissed tonguelessly and retreated another step, its fishlike tail flapping angrily against the flattened remnants of the buildings, suddenly unsure of the situation. Despite the first monster's massive scaly bulk, Raiju was at least twice its size. I doubted it could endure another go-round at this point and not be ripped to shreds.

I smiled, despite myself and despite the horror of the situation. *No mercy*, I thought to Raiju. *Take it apart!*

The great silky ears on the catlike head twitched as if it was listening to my thoughts. The flaming hair on the back of Raiju's neck stood on end like quills, as dangerous looking as the crown of horns on its head that corkscrewed in every direction. It roared at its opponent, the sound so ear-splittingly loud that every window within a thousand yards exploded like a bomb going off.

Raiju leaped, coming down on the retreating monster's muscular fishtail flexing wildly from side to side. Raiju ripped into it, tearing long flaming gouges through scales and skin and flesh. The first monster screamed in pain and tried to leap away, but Raiju had it now and it would not release its prey, raking its claws through the flesh so fiercely that scales flew hundreds of feet into the air to land like burning debris all over the street.

The beast let out a rattling death cry as Raiju worked at reducing it to soft black sludge one swipe of claw at a time. Soon all that remained was a quivering black soup undulating in the middle of the street. The black slime that had once been a kaiju flowed away from Raiju, darting for every grate, open manhole and crack in the street. I jumped back as the slime washed by, singeing the toes of my boots as it retreated into the sewer grate in the curb in front of me. The septic smell of it was enough to make me want to gag in the street.

I thought it would all end there, but bereft of its adversary, Raiju turned its flaming blue eyes on me, belching out rotten-egg-stinking smoke from its flaring nostrils. There was nothing of life or light in those brilliant blue eyes. It looked at me. It listened to me, but it did not love me. It did not even like me. I was less than an insect to it. A bacterium. It had lived a million lifetimes before me and it would live a million more after I was gone. It was a god, after all. It glared at me, challenging me with these thoughts.

How do you approach a god, except on your knees? I felt the massive pressure of its contempt and felt my legs weaken and turn to water, spilling me to the ground in front of the sword. The sword! The sword was responsible, somehow. I grabbed the hilt as the massive Kami towered over me, a fiery brilliance with a grin of saber teeth. I never would have guessed that it hated me so much. The blind, bottomless hatred of angels and demons. It snarled at me, telling me I was stupid and useless. Weak. Telling me to give up, to give in.

I resisted the temptation to beg for my life. I might be ignorant, I might not understand what had just transpired here, but I had never been weak. It was not in my makeup. I had been through too much already. Instead, I used the sword to pull myself to my feet so I was standing against it. It was like standing in a gale-force wind, standing against death or the end of the world, and it was the hardest thing I had ever had to do. If I was going to die tonight, I promised myself it would be as a man on my feet, not a child on my knees.

"I'm not afraid of you," I hissed through my teeth.

You will be, it said, its lightning-blue eyes ripping through me like blades with a single look.

"Oh go to hell," I screamed and yanked the sword from the ground like a modern-day King Arthur pulling Excalibur from the rock. It came out easily, no resistance at all.

The Kami halved its burning eyes at me. I couldn't tell if it was pleased with me or infuriated by my act of insolence. With a flick of its tail, its living coat of fire seemed to go supernova, burning up like a candle flame being snuffed between two invisible fingers. Then it was gone, leaving spots of light and darkness burned against my retinas.

The sword burned up the moment it was free of the ground. Me? I fell down in the rubble of the street, trembling with exhaustion, my hair and clothes smoking coolly. I was still lying there, gagging and shaking like an epileptic some fifteen minutes later when the paramedics finally found me.

4

There's nothing like seeing the inside of the 84th Precinct when you haven't done anything wrong. You know you're innocent, yet you still manage to feel nervous, like they're going to find some dirt on you that even you didn't know existed. I was still messed up after the monster tried to eat me. Being taken down to the precinct to give a statement didn't help much.

A couple of older police officers guided me through a crowded, squalling bullpen to the desk of a young plainclothes detective. I noticed, rather absently that KTV had finally caught up on the events of the evening, though the footage being shown on the TV in the corner of the squad room was strictly ex post facto at this point. The detective started asking me questions, but it took several tries before I was able to answer with any coherency. I felt numb, detached, and had a vague craving for a smoke. He asked me again and again what happened. Again and again, I explained everything while staring wild-eyed at the news broadcast, but after an hour or so, I found myself wallowing in mental Jell-O. I realized I was talking about flaming swords and monsters and other such things that I realized would probably contribute greatly to my long-term commitment to a nice, high-end mental institution.

"...it happened because of the sword...the sword summoned Raiju..."

The young detective looked worried, as if he was afraid I was going to break down into hysterics.

I cupped my hands over my face, feeling like my head was going to explode. I rocked back and forth in my seat. "Mr. Serizawa knew. He knew that Raiju was waking. Somehow. He knew I would summon it with the sword!"

"The...sword?" said the detective. He'd stopped writing my wild shit down a long time ago and just sat there, staring at me with pity-filled eyes.

"The one I made when my hands caught on fire." *Way to go, Kev.*

I was feeling panicky again and I wished I would just shut the hell up. I put my head between my knees and concentrated on just breathing and not passing out as the room swam around me like a giant aquarium. The detective must have seen something in my face because a few seconds later, he was on one knee, holding a wastepaper basket under my chin while I horked violently into it. He squeezed my shoulder, said something about that being enough for now, and I never felt more affection for a stranger than when the officer gave me a paper napkin to wipe my mouth.

He left me to talk to some other eyewitnesses. I stared at the TV as the chattering sounds of the bullpen closed in around me. I had summoned Raiju with the sword, and Raiju had fought the other monster, but none of this was my doing. It wasn't like I had gone out there into the world in search of the magic sword of Castle Greyskull, for fuck's sake.

They'd gotten all they would out of me. I wasn't going to tell them anything. Not until I found out what the hell was going on.

According to the TV, the governor had declared a state of emergency for the City of New York so the National Guard could move in. The part of downtown Brooklyn where the monsters had fought had been declared a disaster zone, damage in the billions. Projects were reduced to smoldering holes in the ground. The club was completely demolished. It was like 9/11 taken to the max.

I wanted my dad. I wanted to get the hell out of here. When I started looking frantically around for an escape, I spotted a group of men in dark suits and coats and plastic-looking hair pushing through the squad room self-importantly. They tripped my trouble radar big time. Definitely not police or plainclothes detectives—you can tell the difference. These guys wore all black and favored designer shades that can't be bought on a cop's salary. I would have guessed FBI or CIA, except they were all Japanese.

I felt a small surge of hope when I recognized the older man in the lead. If I wasn't mistaken, it was steely-haired Dr. Mura of the infamous MuraTech—Aimi's dad. He had made the news often enough that anyone who was a science or Greenpeace geek would recognize him. *Maybe Aimi is here to take me home*, I thought, but I felt my little hope wither away as soon as Dr. Mura stopped at my chair, his coat on his shoulders Mafioso-style. He didn't look like he was here to take me home. He looked like he was here on business.

You should know something. That old joke about all Asians looking alike is totally false. Dr. Mura looks nothing like my dad, even though they're both Japanese and about the same age. Unlike Dad, Dr. Mura is small and fragile-looking, with grey, sunless skin, and myopic eyes behind heavy glasses. My dad is fat and muscular, and he has the kind of open, boyish face that you trust in a heartbeat. You just know he's looking out for your best interest. Dr. Mura, on the other hand, looks skittish, like the little nervous guy in the zombie movie that messes everything up in the end. Standing there beside his tall, muscular men in their dark, undertaker-inspired charcoal suits, a deep crease pulsing between his eyes, he looked less like one of the country's top scientists and more like a put-upon Yakuza kingpin.

I looked up at all the Japanese men standing over me, wondering why Dr. Mura and his goons wanted to talk to me, what MuraTech could possibly want with me. I scrunched back in my seat when a half dozen Dagger shades turned their attention on me. They smiled like mannequins, eyes black and empty like windows to machines. Then they opened fire and the questioning began all over again.

5

Around three in the morning, the MuraTech men finally let me go. By then, I was beyond tired, almost punch-drunk. The windows of the old cinderblock station were pitch black with flickering lights glinting in the darkness beyond—fires. Japantown was burning. I heard sirens as firefighters busily doused the buildings and the surrounding streets. Tomorrow, there might be more. Tomorrow, New York might not exist anymore.

I walked down the long, grubby hall toward the waiting room, past people sitting in cold plastic chairs, crying in groups or alone. I watched babies screaming and old people praying to gods that must have gone blind and deaf to let this happen. I felt numb somewhere in the deeper part of my bones.

I turned my thoughts back to Dr. Mura and his mannequins. Most of the questions had been standard fair, why I was there, what I saw, etc. Nobody asked me about the sword business—I guess they thought I was a crazy boy after what I had witnessed. Something about the MuraTech men were different. They seemed obsessed with every little detail. One even analyzed me by passing a Geiger counter and an analyzing wand over my clothes. I wasn't fooled any. They might have worn dark business suits and glasses, but they all had fancy gadgets and the antiseptic smell of scientists. Their questions were far too detailed for cops or G-men. I'm not as stupid as I look.

"It's a qilin," I told them.

They looked at me in confusion. They might have been Japanese by birth, but they obviously had no idea what I was talking about. The genius IQ comes in handy sometimes. "That's a Japanese chimera, guys. It's made up of all kinds of things— snake, centipede, frog."

They looked even more confused, but instead of explaining, I decided to annoy them some more. "You know, in Japanese mythology, centipedes look like beautiful women before they try to kill you. It couldn't even afford the courtesy."

I was tired and pissed off. Sue me.

The four scientists-in-disguise started grumbling in Japanese, but Dr. Mura killed that with a single look. Gotta love a guy who can give the ol' hairy eyeball. They still looked confused by my assessment but seemed satisfied overall by their findings. Nobody laughed at my joke, but they did let me go after that.

"I hope you catch your monster," I said as I slipped into the remnants of my tattered jacket. I didn't say anything about MuraTech. I knew they were on the payroll, but some stuff is better off if it stays between you and me. I exited stage left without a goodbye.

Out in the hallway, though, Dr. Mura stopped me with a hand on my arm. "I heard you helped my daughter with some bullies," he said, mincing his words not because he didn't know English, but only because it was obvious he didn't use it a lot.

I was surprised by his out-of-freakin'-nowhere statement, let me tell you. I shrugged so he didn't think I was going to be cocky about it. "Yeah, Troy and Zack. They're a couple of jerks."

"My daughter can take care of herself," he growled, surprising me further. "Just leave her alone, Mr. Takahashi."

Ookay.

I stared at Dr. Mura's rock-hard face until he suddenly let go of my arm and stepped back so he could assess me like some new form of bacterium in need of eradication. This was going to take some getting used to. Back in my old school, I was the safe, geeky guy that fathers actually liked when he came to pick up their daughters, fat and harmless. I wasn't used to this new suspicious-parent-ready-to-beat-down-on-bad-boy play, you know? I just backed away, then turned around and wasted no time exiting stage left.

My dad was waiting for me in the reception room, looking more shrunken than ever. I almost didn't recognize him except that he was still wearing his stained cook's whites—complete with deep-fried calamari smell—and a ratty green Army surplus jacket that I would have recognized anywhere. He had gotten it off a relief truck the night San Francisco was leveled, and he'd never parted with it again. He was leaning forward in a cold plastic chair with his hands pressed together as if he were praying, but I knew better. He was remembering, worrying. Obsessing.

He jumped up when he saw me, then just hung there for a second like a puppet without strings. Like everyone else, he didn't know why this was happening, what we had all done to deserve this.

Come to think of it, neither did I.

6

On the ride home things got better in the van, and worse.

Dad drove clutching the steering wheel like a lifeline, downshifting constantly to make the van grip the road that was slicked by all the junk the fire trucks were using to douse the flames in the streets. His face was as impenetrable as a fortress, like he was trying to keep everything from spilling in, or out.

I felt the gnawing need for a cigarette. Biting a dirty fingernail, I turned to the window. The city had sprouted small, random patches of flame that licked upward like monstrous tongues. A derelict car burned. People drifted together to watch a restaurant being doused by the fire brigade. Squads of roving police chased looters away from abandoned shops. A dog howled in response to the never-ending scream of sirens. Great stuff to rattle your nerves. None of the fires seemed to be spreading, but it had taken the firefighters all night to get them under control.

Traffic was detoured around the disaster zone, which stretched twelve city blocks. Traffic being what it was in this town, that meant it was going to be some time before we got home. "Are you sure you're all right?" Dad asked for the zillionth time. He looked me up and down. "I could take you to St. Mary's, if you want."

"The drug rehab center?"

"No, they've converted it into a regular hospital, in case beds are needed."

I thought about that. Not that I needed a hospital, but the implication of needing emergency space made me feel queasy. "I'm all right. Really. I'm tougher than a few bruises."

"I know you are. Mr. Serizawa said you were fine, said he knew it, but I was scared half to death."

"You need to listen to Mr. Serizawa. He's always right."

Dad looked at me as if he couldn't believe I was on Mr. Serizawa's side for a change. He shook his head in wonder. "Why in hell were you there?"

"I...went to see a band at the club."

"Well, why didn't you run when you saw that thing appear?"

I thought about trying to explain about the flaming sword, and the monster I had apparently called from hell, but I had a feeling none of this was likely to float with my dad. At best, he'd think I was hysterical, at worst, insane. I was leaning toward the insane thing myself at the moment. "I guess I froze up." There, that sounded logical, normal, didn't it?

A police car weaved around us, the intense *nee-naw* of the siren clearing a swath through traffic. I envied it. I wanted—needed—to get home. I never wanted a shower so bad in my life. I could still feel the hot alien slime that stank of sewage and evil running down the front of my shirt as Raiju tore Qilin apart. *Asshole monster*, I thought bleakly, *to ruin my clothes like that, even if they were Goodwill fashions.* Even my Harley boots looked like they had been sent through a shredding machine, the leather worn almost all the way through in places.

It was while assessing the damage to my boots that I noticed something near my feet. I picked it up, realizing it was an MLS listing of the kind that you find in waiting rooms everywhere. It was opened to apartment rentals—in Alaska. I got one of my bad feelings which never lied. "Shit..."

"Don't swear," Dad said, all humor gone, "and don't start with me about that, all right?"

"I'm not running again, just so you know."

Dad downshifted stiffly as traffic picked up. He said, softly, ominously, "I don't plan on staying here and watching this city burn down around us. If that thing comes back…" He shivered as he struggled to complete the thought. "I have to think about you. About our safety…"

"I'm not going," I told him, my voice rising a notch. "I'm not running away again." *Maybe*, I thought, *I really was crazy, so shell-shocked from San Francisco I wasn't operating in any kind of reality anymore.* Maybe I was a mental health patient back there somewhere, just drawing a world around me in big colorful Crayolas, a world that never existed outside my own imagination. It sure beat the hell out of the alternative—that I had turned into a superhero with a burning sword and a Kami for a pet.

Dad's jaw tensed, the way mine does when I'm pissed. I could see the tremble in his hands, even in the dark. Fear has a smell, like steel. "Kevin," he said as reasonably as he could. "Look, we're all tired. We'll talk about this in the morning."

The fear, the fatigue, went off inside me like a bomb. I just exploded. I kicked wildly at the dashboard of the van, over and over, like a kid gone berserk. "I'm not running again," I cried, punctuating each word with a good, solid kick of my burned up Harleys. "I'm sick to death of running. Sick to hell of it. Do you think mom would want us running away again?"

I knew it was unfair for me to pull out the mom trump card like that. Thank God we were pulling into the weedy lot that passed for our driveway. I threw the door of the van open before it had even rumbled to a stop.

"Kevin!" my dad yelled, trying to snatch me by the sleeve.

I was sore, tired, so done for the day I felt like crying. I hadn't felt this way since the day they buried my mom and half my classmates in San Francisco. I didn't cry that day, though, and I didn't cry now. I couldn't afford to. One of us had to stay strong.

I was out of the van and into the house before my dad could call me back.

7

Despite the utter and complete exhaustion of my body, I found it nearly impossible to sleep. Too amped, too afraid something would burst out of the ground and the dark underside of my worst nightmares and stare at me with monstrous red eyes.

I took the iPod my dad had given me for my last birthday and lay on the bed, the earphones on, cranking it until I was nearly deafened by "Beethoven's Symphony Number 5," trying not to think, trying not to let my imagination run away with me. I have this insane dream of racing bikes with Beethoven playing over the track. He was so deaf near the end of his life that his music had become violent, almost pathological, and he was one of the few classical Romantic composers who can be heard overtop the sound of a roaring engine. Even Ludwig couldn't drown out the image of the black monster in my head, the screaming, hungry sound it made, or the earth-shattering roar of the creature that had destroyed it.

The creature I had summoned…

I was afraid to sleep, afraid to dream, and in response to that, my brain would not shut down. The music didn't help. The light I had turned on beside my bed didn't help. Nothing helped.

Finally, as the digital clock beside my bed clicked over to 2:30 in the morning, I climbed over Groucho, snoring on the floor beside my bed, and decided to visit Mr. Serizawa in the apartment downstairs.

There was a light under his door. Like a lot of older people, it seems Mr. Serizawa is up all night. To hear him tell it, he hasn't slept in over twenty years. I knocked softly on his door. Anything was preferable to lying in the dark, alone with my music and my rambling, monstrous thoughts.

It didn't take long for him to answer. He pushed the door open, clutching the collar of his jinbei shirt and smiling sadly like he had been expecting me. "*Mago*," he said, "you've come at last."

"Yeah," I said, stuffing my hands in the pockets of my jeans.

"Come in."

I had never been in his apartment before, but it was really freaky, full of low Japanese futons and ornate tables, shoji screens, and smoking samovars. By far, the most peculiar thing of all was the lions. The walls of his apartment were covered in pictures of lions drawn by an enthusiastic but not very talented child's hand. It took me a few moments of intense concentration to realize I had drawn them—that they were my lions. They were from my dad's collection of old drawings from when I was in kindergarten, those that had survived San Francisco and the move. Lions. I used to love lions as a kid—I could never wait to get to the big cathouse at the zoo. I had forgotten.

I looked at the pictures everywhere, then went over to a low shelf where a stuffed lion with wings sat—an old toy of mine that my mom had bought me when I was six years old. I thought I had lost it. I stared in wonder at everything. Mr. Serizawa's entire apartment was like a shrine to my obsession with lions. I picked up the stuffed lion and turned to face him. "How did you get this stuff?" I asked, sounding very accusatory.

Mr. Serizawa didn't seem offended by my tone of voice. "After you and your father moved in, *Mago*, I saw these things in an open box. I asked your father if I could have them, and he said you would not mind. He doubted you even remembered them."

Well, if I wasn't convinced before this that he knew something about Raiju, I was now.

I noticed that he had been watching an old black and white sitcom on late-night television. No KTV. No monsters. Maybe, at his advanced age, Mr. Serizawa no longer feared them. He watched me clutch the lion. He must have read some endless despair in my face, because he immediately shut the television off and said, "*Mago*. I am so sorry." His voice was sad and distant and not like Mr. Serizawa's at all.

I suddenly felt pretty guilty about the child-molester thoughts I'd had about him, but I was also angry. "You knew about it," I cried. I didn't want to say Raiju's name aloud—names have power, at least in the Shinto religion, and anyway, I didn't have to say the name. "How? How did you know about that thing?"

His eyes grew grave and old. "I know because I am a Watcher."

I didn't know what that meant, if anything. "So what does that make me?"

"You, *Mago*, are a Keeper."

I didn't know what that meant, either, but finally exhausted, overwhelmed, I turned my back on him, held my lion, and started to cry for the first time in years.

8

Mr. Serizawa left me alone, allowing me to pull myself together in private. He fixed tea in one of the samovars, then invited me to join him on the tatami mat before his himorogi, a custom-built Shinto shrine.

The boundaries of the shrine were marked with fronds of green bamboo in vases at both ends, between which was strung a large twisted border rope. In the center was a large branch of bamboo, called a sakaki, festooned with various small amulets, almost like a year-round Christmas tree. The sakaki represented the physical and earthly manifestation of the Kami that the devout Shinto worshipped. Hanging from the branches were small wooden animals and jade figurines, a wedding ring that probably belonged to Mrs. Serizawa, coins from different business transactions that Mr. Serizawa had likely considered lucky, some small toys that might have belonged to a child, and finally, several ornate amulets (called ofuda) with kanji inscribed on them. One I recognized as the sacred name. Raiju.

You didn't get all this ethnic information from me, by the way. Remember that.

I knelt there, my hands resting on my knees, and watched Mr. Serizawa preparing rice tea in fragile bisque china cups with no handles. He added some sake to the cups. I tried not to feel tense, but this was ceremonial stuff, done before something of great importance was about to take place—a negotiation, a wedding, or the passing down of an oral tale. I took the cup from him, carefully, properly, and drank with him, swallowing down the tea and sake, which tasted like a combination of vinegar and old gym socks. Uck.

Gradually, the silence between us turned into something else. Mr. Serizawa coughed, shifted uncomfortably, then turned to the shrine. He lit a stalk of cinnamon incense, picked up a small bamboo fan, and cut intricate Kanji characters in the air before the shrine. He began to sing low and intimately in Japanese, something I recognized as a prayer. He drew out the syllabuses, his gruff, aged voice shaping his desire, his exaltation, his plea to the unseen deities of his ancestors—the Kami. It was a very pagan sound.

I shivered as the song ebbed away to silence. He flicked the fan down, then returned to the mat, kneeling stiffly and awkwardly, and said, simply: "Raiju wakes."

I felt a dull stab of shock—this was too much like the dream. I thought again of the monstrous creature with the body of fire and the electric blue eyes—the same color as my own, incidentally. I licked my dry lips, but it still took me two tries to get the words out. "What is...Raiju?" My voice was so low it was little more than a vibration in the air between us. "I mean...that's a god, right? A Kami."

I saw Mr. Serizawa swallow, his throat working. I had never seen him this upset before. It took him a few moments to compose himself, then he centered his attention on me again, hardened his eyes, and said, "The Kami are more than gods, *Mago*. They are the grandfathers of gods. They are the makers of gods, and it is your destiny to be the earthly vessel, the Keeper of the greatest of the Kami. Raiju. The Lion of Fire." He nodded once, dourly. "As it is my destiny, as the Watcher, to bestow upon you the story of the War of the Kami. I have waited a long time for you to find me, *Mago*. A very long time."

"I don't understand," I said. "I don't get any of this."

"I will tell you the story that was told to me by my own grandfather. It is an old story, known by only a few. It is a story that should not be retold except to those you trust with your life. Do you understand, *Mago*?"

"Y-yeah."

He looked at me. Hesitant.

I repeated, in a steadier voice, "Yes, Mr. Serizawa."

I trusted his wisdom. I doubted anything discussed tonight would go over well with my dad—my dad who believed in work, sweat, and all things rational and normal. Mr. Serizawa and I were not here tonight to discuss rational and normal things. We were so far outside the realm of rational and normal that it wasn't even funny anymore.

Mr. Serizawa lowered his head, seemed to gather his thoughts. Then he began to speak.

9

The War of the Kami was told to me on the Island of Itsukushima, near Hiroshima, where my family lived. It was a place I traveled to after the war...after the bombs fell...an old man at seventeen, now fatherless, motherless and wifeless. I went there to speak to my grandfather about what I had done, what I had seen, and what direction my life might yet take. My grandfather was very old, Mago, over a hundred years in age. He was a man of great wisdom. A Shinto priest, he attended to the shrine of Raiju-sama, the Lion of Fire. He would let no one walk near the shrine, lest their footsteps awaken the creature from its deep sleep.

One evening, I had drunk too much sake, and he caught me stepping too close to the shrine. He became agitated. I apologized. In return, he gave me this story to bear and made me a Watcher.

Long before humans walked upon the earth, the Kami crawled and slithered across its surface, and swam in its oceans, and flew across its skies. This was their world then. It was idyllic, for there were no wars to fight, no famine, and the Kami never took more from the earth than what they needed. They never poisoned it in any way, because the earth is the body of Amaterasu, the goddess who gives birth to all life.

The Kami, though peaceful, were also proud creatures. Like gods everywhere, they desired creatures who would worship them, so they gathered together one day and said, "Let us create man."

So it was done, and men were created to live in the green fields of the earth and to care for and worship the Kami, and all was well for a while. But men, who were as proud as the Kami who have created them, became angered when they realized they existed for no other reason than to amuse the Kami. In time, they gathered and said to one another, "It is we who labor and suffer. It is we who should be served by the gods. It is the gods who should listen to our prayers and requests."

They were clever men, and instead of rebelling, they met in secret and devised their plans. "Let us wait and listen, and record the names of all the Kami on metal seals," they said one to another. "Because only when we have written all the names of the Kami on the ofuda, will we then have power over them. We can lock them away in the womb of Amaterasu. Then the earth will be ours."

This took many generations, as you can well imagine. With time and perseverance, the men gathered all the names of the Kami on a great treasure of ofuda. Then came the uprising, swift and brutal. They used the ofuda to strike down the Kami and drive them from the face of the earth. For, you see, to know the name of a god is to have power over it. Some went deep into the sea and became mountains, and some went into the sky and became the stars. Some dug deep into the earth and became the foundations of the greatest cities in the world, and others, the fiercest and most temperamental of the Kami, were driven into hell, the only place that could contain their terrible rage.

Raiju the Lion of Fire was one such beast.

The ones who were confined to hell were the most dangerous, for they would have ripped the heavens apart in their fury. They would have destroyed all that came before to keep it from the hands of men, and there they seethed and the earth felt their wrath in the forms of great storms and lightning.

10

"Do you think any of this mythology stuff is real?" I asked Mr. Serizawa.

Mr. Serizawa said, "Do you?"

He had a point. I wasn't very good at determining reality anymore, so I shut my mouth and just listened.

11

Thousands of years passed, and men became great, far greater than the Kami, for their hands tamed not just the beasts of the earth, but the very elements, as well. After some time had passed, some of the Kami allied themselves with men in order to gain their freedom. They became like tame household pets, serving the very men they themselves had created. That is why we pray to gods and call them by name.

This angered the fiercest of the remaining Kami, and a great war erupted between the Kami who had come to worship mankind, and those who walked the Old Ways and desired an end to their own creation. There was much famine and unhappiness in that time. The War of the Kami nearly upset the balance of the earth before Amaterasu intervened and put the fiercest Kami into a deep sleep within her womb.

Before they slept, the Kami who had given themselves to anger and darkness promised to rise once more, when the time of mankind had begun to wane. In those end times, they swore, after the body of Amaterasu had become polluted and unsalvageable under the ministration of men—and they promised that it would— they vowed to rise, and to take back the earth, or else to destroy it utterly.

12

Mr. Serizawa stopped speaking and only looked long and hard at me. I didn't like that look. It said he believed this stuff a little more than was healthy, but I had to ask it.

"What does all this have to do with me?"

"After the evil Kami were put to sleep, mankind decided it was much too dangerous for the ofuda to remain on earth, where anyone might use them for evil purposes—and yet, they could not be destroyed, either, lest they be needed once more to control the angry Kami. So they were ritually burned and mixed with a potion that was then drunk by the purest of maidens. The ofuda—and thus, the Kami—became part of each of the maidens' wombs and was passed down through countless generations in preparation for the end of days, when the evil Kami would awaken again."

Mr. Serizawa took a deep breath. "The men who had mixed the potion were the high priests, the Watchers who eventually became the tellers of the tale. They—we—wait for the end of days. We know that in the last days, the ofuda will each come alive within a child wizard of pure spirit—a Keeper—and that Keeper will have eyes as silver as the seals with the names of the Kami written upon them, and they will see the wind and call the elements to their aid. They will be burdened with the difficult task of summoning and taming the ancient Kami. This, then, will be the final war. The evil Kami will wish to battle the tame Kami for control of the earth. The rest is left in the hands of the gods—and the children who can summon and control them."

This I so didn't need to hear, though I figured I was an idiot to think it would end any other way. After all, Japan is not exactly known for its cheery, fairy-tale endings.

I had to ask it, of course. "Why...why did your grandfather tell you this story? Why did he make you a Watcher?"

Mr. Serizawa looked at me earnestly. "It was to be my burden to carry for the lives I had taken in the war, and because the end of days is upon us, Kevin Takahashi. The dark Kami wakes, and the Keepers wake with them."

Stupid question. Why do I ask these questions, anyway? Of course, it was something crazy and complicated like that.

Mr. Serizawa said, "You have manifested the sword of fire, yes? You have called Raiju with its sigil?"

I considered telling him everything that happened tonight. It might even make me feel better, but I chose not to speak of it. Not now. To speak of it would make it all real, and I wanted to go on pretending this was a nightmare, at least for a little while longer.

"Why now?" I asked instead, standing up. "Why not a few years from now?" I sounded so bitter. "Why now, for Chrissakes? Couldn't I have at least a few more years of normalcy?" *Really*, I thought, *was that too much to ask?*

Mr. Serizawa looked infinitely sad, as if he could read all my emotions in my desperate face. "You don't understand, *Mago*. You have encountered another Keeper, and it has awakened the Keeper within you. It has awakened the ofuda which dwells in you. You will be drawn to this person. This person will be where you are. The two Kami will now seek each other out, no matter the cost, no matter what you do, or where you go, and battle to the finish."

I glared at him. Another Keeper? I took a quick inventory of everyone I knew who had silver eyes. It didn't take that long. I mean, I had only met one other person in the last few days with pale eyes like mine, and he was currently contemplating kicking my face in. "Snowman?" I nearly shouted. "Snowman controls Qilin? You must be kidding me!"

I couldn't have a normal bully like Troy, or even Bryce, oh no. Not me. Not Kevin Takahashi. Nope. My bully had to be a super-powered freak of nature in charge of a giant, city-smashing slime-o-rama monster with death breath and an even worse attitude problem. Sort of like his master.

I decided then that my life sucked on so many levels I couldn't even count them all anymore.

13

I was late to Biology and had gotten turned around in the school corridor somehow. I had no idea where I was going, but I spotted Aimi up ahead, her plats echoing hollowly in the empty corridors. I started hurrying to catch up to her. At least I could ask her where the classroom was.

"Greetings, Master."

I stopped. Slowly, I turned around.

The Asian woman from my dream stood behind me. She was tall, statuesque, and dressed in a bright red ceremonial kimono flocked with gold, hand-painted flames and birds. She was standing behind me, her hands linked together in front of her wide black obi belt. As I watched, the flames on her kimono seemed to move, to absorb the birds fleeing from them. She was smiling at me with ruby red lips and searing blue eyes. Laughing at me, like I amused her. She was Japanese, yet her hair, done up in hundreds of braids and beads, was as red as my mom's had been, bright fire engine red.

I opened my mouth to say something, to ask what she wanted of me, but she moved forward with lightning speed and reached for me, the elongated, blood red tips of her fingernails brushing my cheek. I noticed there were kanji and other ancient symbols engraved on her nails, each of which was as long and curving as the blade of a short sword. I wanted to back away, but I hit the wall of the corridor. I wanted to cry out, but before I could, her hair burst into a halo of crackling flames that enveloped the entire school corridor—and me.

I lunged awake in bed, panting and heaving with sweat running down my chest under my T-shirt. I took a deep breath and fell back onto the pillows, shaking, my fists bunched up in the bedclothes.

My jaw clenched compulsively as a spike of childish indignation raced up my spine. *I didn't have to be a Keeper if I didn't want to be*, I thought. It was more like a job than anything else, like being a doctor or lawyer or soldier. It wasn't like someone was pointing a gun at my head, making me do these things. This was America, and despite what Mr. Serizawa had said, I could do anything I wanted.

I didn't have to summon the sword of fire.

I didn't have to use the sigil to summon Raiju.

I didn't have to do anything I didn't want to do.

In that moment, I made the vow.

Unfortunately, I must have been more upset than I thought, because the pillow my hands were clenched around went up like a bonfire. I was up in seconds, using the pillow to beat at my hands until the fire was snuffed out.

I didn't feel a thing and my hands didn't seem to be burned, but my heart was racing like a well-tuned V-8 engine in my chest. Jesus, I was turning into that chick in the Stephen King novel on top of everything else, the one who set everyone on fire whenever she had a meltdown.

The pillow was pretty useless when I finished with it. I stuffed it under the bed, hoping my dad wouldn't notice the crispy aroma of fried linen wafting in the night air. To make sure, though, I got out of bed and cranked open one of the industrial windows even though it was a chilly night.

I couldn't sleep. After that, who could?

I locked myself in the bathroom and smoked a cigarette down to a small nub, my hands shaking. I kept expecting to spontaneously combust, but nothing that exciting happened. Finally, I crept out into the hall and visited the kitchen for some oven mittens. I didn't know if it would actually do any good, but I figured it couldn't hurt.

I curled up under the covers, my mittened hands buried under me in an attempt to snuff out any unexpected nocturnal conflagrations.

Then I was able to sleep.

CHAPTER FOUR
Monster Magnet

1

Kevin's list of ways to avoid the end of the world:
1. Clean up the environment.
2. Disarm all nuclear weapons, even those we "don't" have.
3. Avoid all other Keepers at all costs.
4. Start a hug-a-Kami campaign.

I sat at the desk in my room and went over each point with a highlighter. I figured the first two were doable. I just had to become a high-ranking military leader or the President of the United States, whichever came first. Number Three—not so much. According to Mr. Serizawa, Keepers had a weird magnetic attraction to each other, especially now that we were facing the end of days, which pretty much explained why Snowman was like American Express—everywhere I wanted to be. The Kami were actively seeking each other out now, which posed a bit of a problem. I mean, I couldn't exactly run screaming from every person I met who had blue eyes, right? Right?

That left Number Four, and I just didn't think the Kami were the cuddly types, and no, I wasn't being serious with that last one, but I was starting to feel desperate.

"Kevin?" my dad's voice rose up from below. "Where are you?"

"The same place I was an hour ago," I shouted back, then realized Michelle could probably hear me. She'd set up her Netbook in her dad's garage at just the right angle so I could tutor her in tuning up the Interceptor without actually being there.

I glanced at the screen of my laptop and realized she was presently "engaged," as it were. *"Yo mataria tu!"* she barked, throwing down a wrench, which bounced off the cement floor. "Why is the cylinder head not moving?" she asked me with pitiful desperation, rubbing a smudge of grease across the bridge of her nose. "You said it would move!"

I looked over her work. "That's because you're trying to loosen the exhaust port."

"Oh." With a growl and a curse, she turned back to the engine, giving the bike a swift kick.

"Kevin?" my dad shouted. "Do you know where the packaging tape is?"

I let my head drop onto my desk as if it had been decapitated. "The same place it was five minutes ago," I shouted back to be heard over Blue Oyster Cult playing on my iPod. "The kitchen table."

If you asked me what was worse, facing down a Kami from hell or dealing with my spazzed-out dad, my dad would win every time. There are some monsters even a Keeper can't handle. In the days since the attack, he'd barely let me step outside the building to walk Groucho, even though I had tons of time on my hands now.

To quote Alice Cooper, school was out forever…or, at least, until the authorities could prove that no new monsters were going to pop up out of the ground unexpectedly—which was proving difficult. According to the news, the military was sweeping the sewer system, looking for any remnants of Qilin. I didn't think they would find anything. Qilin was toxic slime, basically, and the New York sewers are full of toxic slime.

The no-school thing made everything worse, somehow, because it meant I had absolutely no escape from KTV, or my dad. In the end, I exiled myself to my room, with my stereo turned up on a classic rock station to drown out the incessant babble of KTV, and just my laptop for company, while my dad worked frantically on getting our stuff packed up and getting the apartment in Anchorage.

Thank goodness the web was still working. Were it not for Michelle and Rex, I would have felt like I'd fallen down a hole somewhere.

"I don't suppose you could come over and look at the mess I'm making of this bike, could you?" Michelle pleaded with me. She put her hands on her hips. "I think the patient is dying."

"The patient is not dying," I told her. "You're doing fine. I'll try to come over tonight, after my dad is done freaking, okay?"

Michelle's face instantly lit up.

I felt a little bad about lying to Michelle. I had no idea if I'd be able to make our date or not, what with my dad in a whirlwind of preparations. At the rate he was going, he'd have the apartment by week's end. That meant we'd be gone by next Monday. I didn't know if I wanted to spend time with Michelle and Rex when I might never see them again.

I didn't even know how I felt about that, exactly. On one hand, I was used to the whole lone-wolf routine—I'd grown up an only child, after all, and after my mom had died things had gotten really weird, with my dad sometimes spending days in bed under the covers, clutching her robe, while I was left to my own devices. I liked to think of myself as an island, but I'd gotten kind of used to having Michelle and her brother around, bugging me at school or on the Internet, proving there was an actual life beyond these four walls. Not that I was getting sentimental or BFF-ing or anything like that, because that would totally screw up my lone-wolf image.

I looked at the list I had scribbled and realized it was damned useless. Alaska was starting to look better and better, at this point. *Better I leave now*, I thought, *while I can still cut my losses and not look back.* Not to mention I was finding it somewhat frightening that I could get sentimental over kids I'd only known for a few weeks—that was definitely something old school Kevin would do, and I was totally removed from that crap now.

Fuck it, I thought. I was a total badass loner, always had been, always would be. I flipped down the screen, leaving Michelle to fight with the bike alone, turned off the stereo, and flopped back onto my bed, covering my eyes with my winged lion toy so the sun wouldn't blind me. I listened to the faint morning sounds filtering through the closed window. Traffic on the street, distant sirens, a passing car radio broadcasting a Howard Stern show. Normal city things. Yet nothing was normal anymore.

Last Friday changed the city, the world. It had changed my family. Again.

Another move. A new school. New teachers to hate and new kids to avoid. A new room, with a different angle of sun to burn my eyes. I closed them and gritted my teeth until they ached. I wondered what Alaska was like. I imagined a tiny town floating out on an iceberg somewhere. No girls, no Internet or cable, and a lot of polar bears. Cripes, I might as well be dead. My dad would love it, though—peaceful, white, with no monsters.

Wait: not true. A lot of prehistoric monsters in the movies were frozen for millions of years in the ice of the far north before thawing out and going on a rampage, which didn't bode well. But they would be getting a Keeper, wouldn't they? Kevin Takahashi, Kaiju Hunter, at your service.

I got up and started dressing, just for something to do, stumbling over some textbooks on the floor as I pulled on a fresh pair of jeans and found a T-shirt that didn't smell. The sight of the books made me feel even more depressed, despite the fact that I hated school, the Cinnamonster, everything. I went to the window and opened it to let in some cold morning air and to clear my head. The sky was overcast, threatening rain, and there was a pre-winter chill that made my breath plume. Cars, cabs, and the occasional tour bus moved leisurely up and down the street. Cabbies blared their horns as they competed for early-morning fairs, and a vendor stood out front on the sidewalk, selling bootleg T-shirts and Red Sox baseball caps. Strangely, the world was carrying on as if nothing had happened last Friday. New York was both brilliant and seemingly stupid that way. I wondered what our next place would be like.

"Kevin?" I heard my dad call from the kitchen. "I could use some help with these boxes."

I rolled my eyes. I really needed to get out of here, at least for a little while. Picking up my leather riding jacket and my shades, I discreetly slipped down the backstairs and out the Fire Exit door.

2

The morning had warmed up by the time I reached the gates of The Evergreens Cemetery. Not much, though, and the spiky October air still cut through my jacket like needles as I rode Jennie down the quiet, tree-lined road that wound around a 150-year's worth of granite headstones, marble statues, and chipped, mossy mausoleums.

I didn't know why I was here, only that the road had led me to this place.

The day before, a huge memorial service had been held for the kids who had died in the club, but I hadn't been there to see it, though I'd seen captions in all the major newspapers. I just couldn't bring myself to join the other students in mourning. I don't know, it just didn't feel right, me being there, listening to eulogies from overwhelmed and probably hysterical parents, when I had so much to do with it all.

Maybe I hadn't killed those kids, exactly, but the jury was still out on how much of the disaster was my fault. I mean, if Mr. Serizawa was right, then Qilin had been there at the club that night looking for me. Everyone else had been cannon fodder.

I just couldn't do it, be there. Instead of attending the funeral yesterday, I'd retreated to the rooftop of the Red Panda. There I sat in a lawn chair, despite the fifty-degree weather, and watched the unchanging skyline as I smoked a whole pack of Newports, something I'd never done before. It was my way of mourning, I guess. It was a good thing my dad didn't keep booze or a lot of razor blades around. Who knows what kind of trouble I might have gotten into. After I had chain-smoked the third cigarette, I learned I could light them by just pinching the tips. I'm one talented guy, didn't you know?

Eventually, Mr. Serizawa appeared on the rooftop to tend to the herbal plants he keeps in a miniature greenhouse up there. I ignored him, watching the sun slide down like a pat of butter behind the Empire State Building, though I did hear him say softly in passing, "*Mago*...how are you?"

"I'm great," I answered him, staring at my yellow, nicotine-stained fingertips. "I call demons from hell, can light my own cigarettes without a Zippo, and I burst into flames whenever I get excited. I'm officially a unique person. However, I do plan on asking my dad for a Pyromex anti-flame suit for my next birthday."

I don't know if he picked up on my sarcasm or not. He didn't say anything, just moved on with his little watering can like everything was peachy-keen. Have I mentioned that adults are clueless?

I snorted as I rode past old statues and worn-looking angels, their hands raised in supplication, the road curving toward the center of the cemetery. The new monument was easy enough to spot, so I just looked for the largest collection of wreathes. I parked at the curb and slid my helmet off, hanging it on the handlebars. I noticed a black-clad girl with a bouquet of lilies standing by the granite memorial wall like a shadowy angel of death, her clothes whipping against her body in the sudden high October gales. The rain hadn't broken yet, but the wind was knocking the dry yellow leaves off the trees above, and I watched them seesaw lazily down around her.

I felt a catch in my throat.

I glanced around, half expecting to find Snowman and his band of Whiteface Warriors standing nearby, but Aimi was alone. Steeling myself, I left the bike and started toward the monument.

Aimi glanced up as I approached. She looked thin, transparent, her eyes and mouth were dark smudges in her porcelain white face. She should have looked beautiful, ethereal, but instead, in the whiteface and black makeup, she looked like a big, horrible, Victorian doll come to demonic life. Again I wondered what was wrong with Aimi, what terrible disease was eating through her.

I stopped when I reached the outer edges of the flowers strewn across the massive plot. As far as I knew, none of the kids who had been buried the day before was in Aimi's circle. I had no idea why she was here. Hell, I didn't even know why I was here, except that I felt I owed something to the kids who had died at the club. Maybe she felt the same way.

Our eyes finally met. "You came," she said, an eerie thing to say, like she had expected me to be here, had been anticipating it.

Her eyes flicked up and down. "Did you know any of the students?"

"No. I just...I felt I should be here. Pay my last respects, I guess," I said, stuffing my hands in my pockets. "I keep thinking about those kids caught in the building, what it must have been like for them when they realized they were going to die, when nobody was going to save them and they weren't going to wake up from a bad dream."

"I know." She bent down to set the white bundle of lilies tied with a black ribbon down, and then glanced at the names of so many of our classmates engraved on the wall. She let out her breath. "I keep dreaming about it."

I waited, letting the moment linger, until Aimi lifted her head and broke the silence. "Kevin, are you staying in the city?"

I kicked at some loose gravel. More than half of the city had already been evacuated or were in the process of taking off. Most were heading for New Jersey, Pennsylvania, anywhere they thought, or only hoped, was safe. I felt too ashamed to admit that my dad and I were a part of the panicked majority that were working on leaving. "Yeah," I finally fibbed, then felt really bad. "I mean...we're going to leave eventually. Soon, I guess. Are you?"

She shook her head. "My dad has to stay to clean up this mess."

That made sense. "He's keeping you here?"

I saw a shadow pass behind her eyes. Her face became hard and suddenly very old, almost haggard. "He always keeps me with him." She shrugged. "My mom died when I was born. It's always been just the two of us, and he's...excitable. Daddy always needs to know where I am."

"Sorry," I said, feeling like I'd crossed some invisible line. "I just figured he'd send you away. Someplace safe. I mean...it's a dad thing, don't you think?"

"Maybe," Aimi sighed, suddenly sounding angry, "but I can't go ten feet without him. Without being watched constantly."

Unfortunately, I knew what she was talking about.

She nodded at some trees. "Take a look."

I pushed some professionally trimmed fir trees aside. On the other side of the hill was a long, paved road, and a slick black limo waiting at the curb, with a chauffeur leaning against the driver's side, reading a newspaper. I would have been seriously jealous about Aimi's ride, except that the chauffeur looked exactly like the MuraTech men who had interrogated me at the police station. I swear, Dr. Mura's MIB clones were everywhere, and they all looked alike. I wondered if there was a big machine somewhere that just stamped out the same thing over and over.

Maybe, I thought, *being rich wasn't so great.* Especially if it meant your parents were even more psycho about watching you than my dad was.

Aimi turned, her gestures almost mechanical, and brushed down her long black mourning dress. She glanced over to my side of the street where Jennie was parked. "It must be great being able to go where you want, when you want to."

"It's okay," I said. I didn't bother to mention that I was sort of grounded forever after that little escapade the other night.

She started toward the road, glancing furtively over her shoulder as if she were afraid there were MuraTech men hiding in all the bushes, waiting for her to step out of line. When she reached the bike, she ran her hands over Jennie's handlebars with exaggerated care. "Kevin," she said, turning her coal-black eyes on me, her expression suddenly young and yearning, almost desperate. "We don't have much time left. Will you take me for a ride into the city?"

3

"Don't you want to change?" I asked as I reached for my helmet. I turned to look at Aimi, the elaborate, frothy lace dress, the ribbons in her hair, the long, lace black gloves. I looked at her pale, stoic face.

She glanced over to where I knew the limo driver was pouring over the Sunday odds on the opposite side of the hill. She put a lacy finger to her lips. "What I want is to get out of here," she whispered. Gathering her skirts, she slipped into the saddle behind me as easily as if she were dressed in jeans and a tee, and slid her hands around my waist. It was a really good feeling.

"Won't you get in trouble?" I said, not that I was opposed to the idea of taking a hot girl into the city, but I'd had a lot of experience with spazzy parents of late.

"Do you really care?"

"Do you?"

She put her mouth very close to my ear. I could almost taste her perfume. Like, wow. "Just ride, handsome," she said.

I kicked Jennie to life and listened to the familiar beat of her old V-4 engine turning over, kicked the brake stand up, and cruised out into the street, conscious of the extra weight on the bike. I took her slow at first, but pretty soon, the three of us found our groove. Jennie was an ugly bike—nothing like John Woo would use, whatever Terry thought—but Wayne had been a mechanical genius, and true to his legacy, she rode like an angel.

"Where do you want to go?" I said.

"Anywhere!" she said, sounding breathless. "Just go!"

We cruised through the downtown Brooklyn Garden District, the wind flicking through our clothes and hair. With half the city gone, the streets were practically all ours. Aimi wrapped her arms tight around my waist, and it wasn't long before she rested her head against my shoulder and I could smell the strawberry of her shampoo. We passed old brownstones and empty parks, crumbling theatres and churches full of the devout praying for deliverance. Out on the street, the remaining people were packing their belongings in cars for their extended trip out of the city, or, if they didn't have transport, backpacking it out of there. They looked up as we cruised by, probably trying to figure out why the Revolutionary France chick was riding with the punk kid, but I didn't care. We didn't care. For the moment, at least, the city was ours.

We were halfway down a tree-lined street (trees do grow in Brooklyn, by the way, however stunted) when Aimi lifted her head at the sound of heavy metal being played at roughly the volume of a nuclear explosion, and tapped my shoulder. I slowed the bike as we came upon an old two-story saltbox that had somehow retained its shingles despite the earth-shattering pounding of the bass beat emanating from within. There were a circle of kids camped out on the front lawn, drinking and smoking doobs, and above them, hanging from the eaves of the porch, was a homemade banner that proudly proclaimed: QILIN, WE WELCOME U TO NYC!

From my time in San Francisco, I knew immediately what it was: a monster party. Let me explain. You know those hurricane parties you always hear about down in Florida, where a big group of people stand around in glass buildings, getting blitzed and waiting for the storm to hit and make them all martyrs? Yeah, you got it.

As I pulled to the curb, one of the stoners in a stocking cap immediately stood up and swayed toward us, grinning maniacally and clutching the neck of a bottle of Wild Turkey. "Hey, man, glad you could make it!" he screamed over the music pounding from the house like he knew us, was expecting us. He extended his smoke. "Take a hit, man," he said, "makes you mellow."

I really wasn't into that—I mean, I'm not *that* corrupt, at least not yet. I looked over, afraid Aimi might take up his invitation. Since she was richer than God, she probably knew more about recreational drugs than anyone at school. I found to my relief that she was shaking her head. The kid looked crestfallen. Aimi looked over the group. "What are all you doing here? Shouldn't you be leaving the city?"

"There's nowhere else to go, and pretty soon, we'll all be dead anyway," said the stoner with a shrug. He pulled his wool cap down halfway over his eyes and squinted up at the sky like he expected it to start raining stones at any moment—or monsters. "Fuck it. Might as well enjoy yourself while you can."

I looked over at the other stoners who were presently engaged in a deep, philosophical conversation about which borough Qilin ought to wipe out next, the Bronx or Brooklyn. The Bronx was winning more votes because Brooklyn had better pizzerias—and felt an annoying pang of sympathy. It was pretty obvious from their appearances that they were way too poor to leave the city. Like most folks in the projects, they were stuck here and forced to make do while the military did its best to root Qilin out of the sewer system—if, indeed, they could.

Aimi took my hand and pulled me away, leading me inside the house. The minute we stepped inside, we were assaulted by heavy metal being played at such a high volume that I thought the bones inside my body were going to crumble. Mind you, I like loud music, and I like metal as much as the next guy, but you reach a point when it's so loud there's no music left, just one long ongoing cacophony. We were way past that point. Now, add that to about five dozen kids screaming at each other in order to be heard overtop it. Then throw in the sound of explosions from a group of kids playing *Grand Theft Auto* on a widescreen television in the living room, the shrieks of a half dozen, half-dressed and extremely high girls chasing each other around the room with cans of Redi Whip, and about a dozen guys clay pigeon-shooting with the house flatware and a couple of BB rifles, and there you had it. It was like Dante's version of hell, for teenagers.

Aimi seemed to like it, though. I guess it was a big change from what she was used to. After seeing the stretch limo, I could imagine her dad dragging her to dull dinner parties full of Waterford crystal and boring rich banker guys in tuxedoes, who drank dry martinis and talked about their stock investments. I think that in the Land of the Rich, burping at the table is probably a hanging offense. She moved from room to room, staring at everything in wide-eyed wonder.

I really couldn't blame her. It was my first "adult" party too. I mean, I'm not Rebecca of Sunnybrook Farm. I didn't think it would be kids playing Twister, drinking Kool-Aid, and watching Disney movies on TV. I just wasn't ready for the oceans of booze that were flowing, or the number of kids who were high and cackling, or the incredibly diverse number of drugs that were being passed around as party favors—by a candy striper, no less. As we passed through the rooms, we saw a buffet on the dining room table—greasy open pizza boxes and half empty buckets of fried chicken, and about two dozen empty and mostly-empty bottles of hard liquor rolling around the tables and on the floor. On the sofa were three or four kids making out, all together. I mean, you could have filmed an episode of *Girls Gone Wild* here. I wasn't used to this scene.

Everyone appeared to be having fun, but at the same time, it was a pretty dismal scene, like everyone knew it could only end one way—with Qilin's arrival—and they were going to get in as much life as possible before it was all snuffed out.

Down in the den it was minimally quieter—the noise was down to about the level of an earthquake. A bunch of kids were playing pool in the corner, trying to bounce the balls off the velvet, while the real study-hounds and geeks had gathered around a TV and were glued to an address by the Pope about the End Times and the rise of Satan in the form of kaiju.

Aimi and I stood in the doorway and watched. There was a cutaway of a choir of school-age children assembled in the middle of St. Peter's Cathedral, candles in hand, singing hymns. Aimi took a deep, shuddering breath at the sight of the vigil, her shoulders rising and falling. "What if Qilin really is a demon, Kevin?" she said. "What are we going to do when it comes back?"

I thought about taking her aside and telling her about Raiju—and about the Keepers. About Snowman and his control over Qilin, but if I said that, she might think I was making it all up just to hurt Snowman in her eyes. Anyway, how could I expect her to believe anything so wild like the Keepers? This stuff was insane even to me.

I had to say something. The longer she hung with Snowman, the more danger she was in. Qilin could rise at any time, and the last thing I wanted was Aimi caught in the middle of our little war. I was about to open my mouth when a cue ball came out of nowhere and hammered me in the shoulder, hard. I turned, ready to lay into the dumbass who'd jumped the ball my way...then recognized one of the pool players in the corner as Troy.

He stood up, twirling the cue stick in one hand like he thought he was Mr. Kung Fu, while Zack stood like a brick wall behind him, doing the whole lackey backup thing. Ever notice that bullies always have backup? It's like they can't quite do it all on their little own.

I massaged my sore shoulder, trying not to look too surprised. I was still doing better than Troy, with his bandaged nose and most of his face swollen a deep purple. He looked like he'd tried to make out with a truck going 30 miles an hour—and failed. Oh man, I was so dead.

"You," he said, but it sounded like Munchkin talk with his nose all messed up. "What are you doing here, dead man?"

I thought about going up to him and punching him in his already-broken nose. Nah, that would make his friends beat me to death with their pool cues. I decided instead on the dignified response—apologizing and turning around and guiding Aimi out of the house. Except, when it came right down to it, I did neither. I said, "When did they let you out of the zoo, Troy? Won't your handlers be missing you?"

Aimi covered her mouth with both hands to stifle a laugh.

I admit, I could have handled things better than this, but there was just something about Troy that pissed me off on a deeply primal level. A psychologist would probably have said I was working out my past aggressions with Bryce, since I would never get a chance to settle things in person with him. They might have said I have issues, but I like to think it was the nauseatingly cocky look on Troy's face, despite the broken nose. That and the fact that Troy was just plain stupid. I mean, do you need to be humiliated twice in front of your peers before you learn to back down?

"You got some guts for a yellow chink," said Troy.

That's an approximation, by the way. His words were way more garbled than that and were enunciated in Munchkin-speech, but I figured it out. And that's another thing. Kids like me have been clashing with kids like Troy since probably before the Stone Age, and yet, the taunts and name-calling never get any more creative. It's always about being different from the core group, but then, I'd been hearing that crap since kindergarten, when kids stopped being kids and started being prejudice like their parents. The Asians never felt I was good enough to join their little reindeer games, and the whites think hanging with me will slant their eyes.

Okay, I admit it. I have anger-management issues. Happy?

"Guts," I reminded him, "and an unbroken nose, dumbass."

If he were a cartoon character, steam would have poured out of Troy's ears with the sound of a whistle. Zack was slightly more subtle: he cracked his knuckles and grimaced as if someone had stuffed his mouth full of Sour Patch Kids.

They looked at each other, then glared at me with collective hatred. Now, this scene I was used to. Gripping their pool cues in white-knuckled fists, they swaggered over to beat the crap out of me.

4

"Kevin, what if you could stop Qilin?" Aimi said. She was standing beside me in the holding cell of the 84th Precinct, and she said it with a lilt in her voice.

My stomach flipped over, though that had nothing to do with the various aches and bruises that Troy and Zack had bequeathed me. Still, I wondered how she had read so close to my rambling, ongoing thoughts. I leaned my forehead against the bars of the drunk tank and stared at my feet.

"I mean…what if you knew something that the military didn't, but it would hurt you to tell them? Would you still do it?" she asked, turning to look at me with dire eyes. "Would you do anything to stop it? Anything at all?"

I wondered if she knew about Snowman, and if so, would she defend him, even knowing what he was…what he was capable of?

"You were in San Francisco," she persisted. "You know what can happen. What would you do?"

My mouth was suddenly so dry it took me a couple tries to find my voice, but I told the truth anyway. "I'd do whatever I had to do to protect those around me."

Her hand sought mine, took it, like that night behind the club. Her hand had been so weak and cold then. Tonight, though, there was strength in her grip, and hard chips of determination in her eyes. "Thank you," she said, and reached up and kissed me on the cheek, making me wince as she hit a sore spot.

"For what?"

"For tonight. For everything." She drew back, and I saw her eyes: black, fathomless, almost surreal in her deathly white face. They looked like portals of black glass. She pressed her hands prayerfully together. "This was the best night of my whole life!"

I lifted an eyebrow at that. "*This* was the best night you've ever had?"

Aside from the usual drunks smelling of vomit, there were a bunch of kids in here with us, sitting despondently on bunks or standing around with their hands in their pockets, looking like they were waiting for the hangman to come for them. All of them looked bruised and slightly smashed by the night's adventure. I probably looked worse than any of them. Well, Troy and I— except Troy was gone. His grandmother had shown up ten minutes ago in her housecoat and babushka, all three-hundred-pounds of her, and had literally beat him with her right shoe out of the cell and down the hallway to the exit, while Troy cried, "Gramma, Gramma, I'm sorry, Gramma!" I had a feeling Gramma would be finishing up with Troy at home, and that Troy would soon be sporting new bruises.

I figured my sentencing couldn't be far behind. It had taken four squad cars' worth of police to break up the fight at the monster party, which had acquired a certain surreal quality about it, complete with broken pool cues, broken furniture, a broken liquor cabinet that had drenched me in cheap scotch, and a stereo system that went kaput when I shouldered Troy into it. It had been a pretty colorful fight, and had garnered a nice audience for us, but the owners of the house, assuming they were still in the city, would not be happy campers when they saw how we'd redecorated their den.

In a way, it had been fun, even though I felt like I'd been dragged behind a small truck, and I wasn't exactly looking forward to the consequences.

"I thought maybe this was like every Saturday night with Snowman," I said, then instantly regretted it. *Way to go, Kev. Jealous, much?*

Aimi glanced around the station. Most of the cops from the night Qilin first attacked the city were on duty tonight. Most were staring at me like I was the Antichrist descended to earth. I really couldn't blame them. Every time some drama broke out in this town, I seemed to be at the center of it. Hell, even I would have been suspicious of me, at this point. "Snowman and I have fun," she said. She looked around at the station. "But not like this. The way everyone is staring, I think you're some kind of celebrity."

I poked at a loose tooth at the back of my mouth with my tongue. "So is he." A part of me again wondered if I should blurt out my suspicions or keep them to myself.

She gave me the drollest look. "Snowman and I are best friends, Kevin, and nothing will ever change that. Believe me, you're worried over nothing." I must have looked unconvinced, because she added, "Snowman has his sights set on someone else, just so you know."

I was about to try and puzzle that one out—how Snowman could notice anyone past Aimi—when I heard footsteps approaching and turned to see Dr. Mura standing in the station, dressed much the same way as last time. He glared at me as he clutched the collar of his coat closed. Suffice to say he didn't exactly look like my number one fan. "You," he said. The ice in his voice could have frozen a bonfire.

Aimi's face turned hard. "Daddy...it wasn't Kevin's fault! He didn't start it."

I did finish it, though.

Dr. Mura kept his hairy eyeball on me as he approached the drunk tank.

"Daddy...!"

"That's enough, Aimi. We'll talk about it when we get home."

A duty cop stepped forward to let Aimi out of the tank.

I felt a sudden spurt of anger somewhere inside. I think it was a case of hero-itis...or maybe stupidity. "It wasn't Aimi," I hurriedly told Dr. Mura. "It was all me. Aimi had nothing to do with tonight, with any of this..."

"Oh," said Dr. Mura, "I know that." He glared in at me, looking like he wanted to reach through the bars and pull me through by the hair. Under the circumstances, I probably had that coming. "I specifically told you to leave my daughter alone. Yet you disobey me. Just who do you think you are, young man?"

The voice of parental authority. The old Kevin would have shrunk down to roughly microscopic size. Me, on the other hand...

"Well, I'm not one of your lackeys, that's for sure," I said. "Where do you get those guys?" I said, indicating the zombie standing next to him. "Do you farm them like vegetables or just manufacture them? Do they actually have eyes?" I took a step forward but a cop held out his hand to keep me from stepping outside the cell. "Just dump the condescension and get out of my face, old man!" I shouted.

Way to go, Kev. Forget about having Dr. Mura as an in-law. Like, ever.

Dr. Mura looked taken aback by my baditude. First surprise, then anger crossed his face—the kind, I should add that usually lands people in maximum security prisons for life for first-degree murder. I imagined he was contemplating whether he could choke the life out of me before a cop pulled him off of my gasping, slowly dying body. He narrowed his eyes to black slits. "Last warning," he said evenly. "You'll get no more from me. Next time I act."

I took a step back, feeling like I was being shoved by the force of the anger in his voice alone. Act? Act as in what? What could he do to me? Shoot me?

Without another word, Dr. Mura started down the corridor, his hand guiding Aimi along as if she were an invalid, but before she left with her father, she whipped around and ran back to the cell and took the bars in her hands. She took a deep breath, the bodice of her dress rising and falling. "I'll do what I can to clear you of all this," she promised. "I'll tell them it was Troy that started it." Then her fact crumbled. "I'll see you soon, Kevin."

I sat down on a bunk. I looked into her eyes and recognized the dark truth there. She was lying. I licked my lips, tasting the blood from my broken lip. "There won't be a 'soon'," I said, my voice pitched low so she wouldn't hear the sound of it trying to crack. Like that first time behind the club, there was a lump in my throat, but for an entirely different reason. This time around, I knew it was over before it ever began. I was saying goodbye.

"No," she said, staring at her feet, "I guess there won't." Her voice was small and trembling, full of unshed tears. Finally, she looked up, her eyes shining. "You have to understand, Kevin, my dad…"

"Fuck your dad."

She trembled. "I wish…" She blinked against the tears welling up in her eyes. "I wish it were that easy."

If wishes were horses, and all that. "I'm not good enough," I said, the words just jumping right out of my mouth the way they had a tendency to do of late. I saw her flinch, and experienced a miserable moment of utter satisfaction. "That's it, isn't it? Not white enough, not yellow enough...not rich enough..."

"It's not that, Kevin."

"Then what is it?" I realized I was shouting and making the cops on duty nervous. I didn't want to lose it, not like I always did, but trying to hold it in was like trying to stop a nuclear explosion by stuffing the bomb inside a hatbox. It just wasn't going to happen.

"You don't understand."

"No," I said, slumping back, "I guess not."

"Kevin...please...please don't be angry."

"Not hearing you." I looked around at all the other miscreants. I figured I'd better get used to it. I had a feeling I was going to be here a while. Who knows, it might even be a way of life, the way things were going. Anyway, I belonged here, not in Aimi's ivory tower of a life. Who was I kidding?

"I am *so* sorry, Kevin," Aimi said, grasping the bars separating us. "Today meant so much to me. More than you'll ever know." When I didn't answer, she finally turned and left me to stare at the cinderblock walls.

I was so done with this romance shit.

5

My dad showed up around five in the morning to take me home. This was the second time he was picking me up at the police station, and he wasn't thrilled, to say the least, but at least he didn't say anything as I climbed gingerly into the van, a hand over my bruised ribs. I slid the door closed with an audible clunk. I didn't feel like talking. I didn't feel anything. I just wanted to get the hell away from the station as soon as possible.

My dad looked me over like he didn't recognize me. "You okay?"

I guess I looked pretty busted up. The truth was, it hurt with every breath I took. It hurt to just think, and I wasn't all right. I was as far from all right as anyone could be. I sat back gingerly in my seat. "Just drive, Dad," I whispered.

"That's me," he said, gripping the steering wheel with white knuckles. I saw his jaw clench, the way mine does when I'm ticked. "Dad the chauffeur."

I touched my head where a headache was growing exponentially worse by the second, like bass drums inside the walls of my skull. It probably had something to do with the fact that it was there that Troy had landed his stick. I thought about telling him everything, but if he knew what I was mixed up in, he'd go ballistic—if he believed me at all. He'd probably lock me in my room until I was thirty years old. "You want I drive?"

"That's not what I mean," he said, low, voice grating.

Here it comes, I thought. I should have known to expect something. This time there would be no pass Go, no collect $200. I was good and well screwed with my dad. I decided to give it the final push. I don't know why. Maybe because I hated myself that much. "What do you mean? I mean…what do you want from me?"

Dad shook his head as he pulled into the street and downshifted violently, grinding the gears. "I don't know. Maybe for you to stop acting like an ass and running after girls, sneaking out and partying and boozing it up. That would be a good start," he said, nodding to himself.

"I'm not acting like an ass." Real lame. I fiddled with my glasses. "Shit."

"You know, you don't have to play act the tough-guy image all the time," he said, glancing over at me with a sour look on his face. "I get a call you're at the station…again. You scare the living hell out of me. You get into a fight with some punk. You smell like alcohol…" Again, he shook his head. "This isn't you. I feel like I hardly know you anymore, Kevin."

That lump again in my throat. My heart felt like a stone, like it didn't belong in my chest. I could think of a thousand retorts. All of them would get me in deeper with my dad. Some of them would even make him afraid of me. I was tempted. I was feeling self-destructive again, but I kept my big fat mouth closed. *Just let it be*, I thought. *Let him get it out and over with.*

"What is going on with you lately? It's like you're somebody else. Somebody I don't know."

I tried to ignore his words.

"Is it that girl?" he asked. "If it's some girl getting to you..."

"It's not a girl, Dad."

"Then what? What the hell's the matter with you? You were a good kid, once. A genius..."

A genius who was a wimp, a loser.

"I know things are rough right now. I know how you feel, but I'm doing the best I can..."

I let out my breath in a puff. Enough. "You have no idea how I feel, okay?" I shouted at him, surprising myself. My voice sounded course, like I had whatever Snowman had. "You have no idea what I'm going through right now, so don't talk to me like I'm a retard or a crazy, all right? *Fuck.*"

He looked at me, blatantly shocked by my words. He opened his mouth, then closed it as he turned his attention back on the road. We inched down the crowded avenue. The air inside the van became stifling, electric. "I wish your mom was here," he said at last. "She was always better with this stuff than I was. She, at least, could talk some sense into you..."

"Mom's gone," I spat. "She's dead. Get over it already!"

He hit me backhand style, knocking the glasses off my face.

It wasn't a hard hit—I barely felt it at all, I was so numb from everything else that hurt. But my dad had never hit me before, not when I was little, not while I was growing up, and no matter how big of an asshole I was being. It stunned me and put me in a surreal place. I was actually surprised to feel the nasally onslaught of tears in my eyes and nose.

I looked at him. An old man. I looked at my dad for the first time not like my dad, but like an old man crumbling away under one too many disasters. I realized he was frightened, a husband without a wife, a father who didn't even know his own son, a dirty, tired little man stinking of fried fish who didn't know if the world was going to fall in around him tomorrow. I looked at him and saw just how lonely and shrunken he really was.

That's what frightened me more than anything. He had no more power to protect me than the military, which couldn't stop all the monsters in the world from rampaging. Only I could do that. The great and mystical Keeper.

The van was stuck in traffic. I picked up my glasses and reached for the door.

"Kevin..." he said.

I shrugged off his hand and opened the door and jumped out, slamming the door of the dirty little van stuck in traffic with my dirty little dad in it who looked so confused by everything. I climbed over the medium and headed for the shoulder of the road, weaving through the motionless traffic full of dirty little people who didn't know if they were going to live or die.

When I reached the edge of the street, I turned around and saw my dad standing beside the open door of the van. He was calling me back while cars and trucks honked impatiently at him from every angle, but I kept walking away.

6

When I was younger, and my dad pissed me off—it didn't happen often, but it did happen—I sometimes fantasized about running way. Just taking my backpack and walking in no specific direction until adventure found me, a real modern day Tom Sawyer. Just one without a raft or a Huck Finn.

I never would have really done it; that's why it was only a fantasy.

I never thought I would actually go through with it, until now. I made my way through Brooklyn Heights, past old historical neighborhoods full of fading brownstones, novelty shops, bistros and open-air kiosks with no one at the helm, I started wondering if I had made the best decision. In the greasy yellow light of morning, the place looked deserted. Shops were empty and the streets felt weirdly apocalyptic. Most of the neighborhood had been evacuated sometime during the night. There were cars dead in the streets and newspapers scattered across the cobblestone sidewalks with big marketable banner headlines like NYC AWAITS GIANT MONSTER ATTACK!

I walked until my ribs started hurting so badly that I was forced to stop and rest in front of a trade-in furniture store window where two teenaged looters were loading TVs onto a pickup truck. KTV was playing in triplicate on the TVs in the window, and a stringer from the Kaiju Network was announcing an impending quarantine of the city. Soon, no one would be allowed in or out as the military attempted to trap Qilin in the sewers. I watched the boys load the goods up onto a truck, each of the TVs dying as their plugs were pulled and they were duck-walked up the ramp of the truck. After high-fiving each other, one ran around to the driver's side and got in, turning the engine over. It was only then that they realized what I had first noticed on approaching them—they were gridlocked in dead traffic, cars and buses parked every which way in the street when people took off on foot, with no way to drive off with the loot.

I moved on, a cynical little smile on my face. Eventually, I found myself at an intersection with a broken stoplight that looked like it had been shot out. An un-New York silence hung over the street, except for the distant popping sound of gunfire as a conflict erupted a few blocks down. If more looters were about to hit town, I didn't want their kind of trouble. I had enough of my own.

I crossed the street and ducked inside a drug store that seemed to be open. Inside, people were haggling with the pharmacist, trying to get prescriptions filled if they could before leaving town. It felt nice to be inside the store, normal. I sat down on a bench and reached for some painkillers on a nearby rack, dry-swallowing four caplets. KTV played in the corner, the newscast illustrating how each borough of New York was being systematically evacuated. I tried to decide what to do.

If I hunted down Snowman, even if only to try and reason with him, our Kami would be forced to duke it out in the streets, and if I ran away, Qilin might follow me. Damned if you do, damned if you don't. Either way, I was damned.

The painkillers helped, but they also made me feel incredibly tired. I decided to close my eyes for only a second, but a second was all it took.

7

"Aimi," I said, walking after her in the school corridor. I had finally caught up to her. I touched her shoulder.

Aimi turned around, but I realized, belatedly that it was the woman from the dream several nights ago who stood there in the halls of our school. She was wearing the same type of kimono, red silk that seemed to breathe, with flames dancing along the sleeves and hem like weird movie CGI. She smiled, and her teeth were long and white and almost painfully sharp in her rose red mouth. *Master*, she said, though her lips didn't move at all. She licked her wet red lips with a long black tongue. She unfolded her arms, and I saw that beneath her draping sleeves she held Aimi in her grip, her long painted nails stretching across Aimi's white, painfully frightened face. *For you, Master*, said the woman in the kimono, and with those words, she plunged her long catlike claws deep into Aimi's heart.

Aimi's eyes flew wide open, brimming with a sea of black tears. Aimi screamed.

I jerked awake. I knew it was a dream—had known for some time while still in the dream—but that didn't make it any less painful. It had felt so real that I felt compelled to glance down at my hands, afraid they had sprouted flames again. They were long and white and heavily corded, the nails bitten pitifully short, but normal.

"Excuse me. Son?"

It was the voice that had awakened me. I jerked around guiltily.

A tall, beer-bellied security officer was standing over me, a police ban radio squawking on his belt. I wondered if he had seen me swiping the painkillers, or if it was something else that had put me on his trouble radar. Maybe my dad had gone to the police and had an APB issued for my whereabouts. That was practical, and it was something he would have done. The guard looked me over as if he were trying to see past the glasses. "Is your name Kevin Takahashi?"

I stared back at him with my patented blank look. He was looking for a blue-eyed Japanese kid. He couldn't see past the rosy Ozzy glasses, and thanks to my mom's genes, I didn't look Japanese with my face completely relaxed. "No," I said. "No, officer."

"You wouldn't happen to have a license or an ID on you?"

Great. I fiddled with the glasses. "Sure," I said, reaching into my jeans pocket, trying to figure out what to do next. If the police hauled me back to my dad, I wasn't sure what would happen.

No, that was a lie. I knew exactly what would happen. Qilin would find us both, and there was no way I was going to let that happen.

A commotion suddenly broke out at the pharmacy window. Two old women had started wrestling over a bottle of pills. The bottle popped out of their hands, caplets scattering like loose teeth across the linoleum. I nodded at them. "Better take care of that, officer."

The security guard swore under his breath and turned to attend to the row.

I exited stage left and was halfway down the street before the door had finally closed behind me.

8

I walked, and as midmorning gave way to noon, I started ransacking my jacket pockets. Even a piece of gum would have been welcomed at this point, but my pockets were torn and empty. I wondered if other Keepers had to contend with being cold and hungry all the time, or if I was just a special case.

I spotted a vending machine across the street, next to a news kiosk with yesterday's news stacked in neat, untouched rows. I almost kicked myself for not thinking of it sooner. I charged across the street and sank four quarters into the machine, then pushed a random button, pushed it again. Nothing. I tried another button, but the results were the same. Then I noticed the lights on the machine were off. All those machines, and none of them were working. Water, water everywhere and all that good stuff. I stepped back and collapsed in the gutter, watching garbage flutter back and forth across a sewer grate.

All at once, I started to cry like a baby.

I just cried and cried there on the empty street corner, amidst the stalled traffic and tall, unseeing buildings, and the machines that no longer worked in a city that was probably going to be destroyed soon anyway. I didn't know where I was going, what I was doing. I wanted my dad. I wanted my mom. I wanted Wayne, and San Francisco. I wanted to go home. My ribs hurt. My heart hurt, and I was just so sick of everything. So sick of holding everything back, of being strong, of being an adult. I didn't want to be an adult. I wanted to be a kid because that's all I was, and I wanted to have a tantrum, and break something, and swear, and cry, and it wasn't fair that I should have to do this, any of this...

Dammit.

I cried until there wasn't any more, until it was all used up, and then I just sat there on the curb, wiping my nose, thinking cynically, *Well, that was useful. That accomplished a lot.* I took a deep breath, took my shades off and wiped my eyes, wishing I had someone to talk to, some idea of what to do, where to go. I was alone. More alone than I had ever been in my life.

When the first faint strains of "Fur Elise" reached my ears, I had no idea what was happening. I thought maybe I really had lost it. Then I remembered that I had programmed that into my phone. I'd forgotten because no one ever called me. I didn't even know why I carried the damned thing around, except that my dad was a total stickler about me having a phone.

I picked it up and looked at it. It wasn't my dad calling—though there were a number of missed calls, probably from when I was asleep—my frantic dad trying desperately to get in touch with me. I didn't recognize this number at all. I squinted at the phone as a bad feeling started churning in my gut that had nothing to do with the weird dream about Aimi or the utter, overwhelming despair I was feeling at the moment. I hit the button and licked my dry lips—they felt numbed and wind burned like I'd taken a massive hit of Novocain at the dentist's—and said, "Umm...yeah?"

All I could hear was a raspy breathing on the line. I set my jaw. If this was a prank or some telemarketer or something...

"Who is this?" I demanded.

"Kevin?"

I jerked. "Snowman?"

There was a long pause, and for a moment, I wondered if this was a dream, or if I was just imagining that my arch-nemesis was calling me on my cell. Maybe he'd called to gloat? He was definitely the type. "Kevin...man, I'm sorry to be calling you like this."

Snowman apologizing? Now I knew something was up.

"How did you get my number?" I asked, thinking maybe Aimi had given it to him, or he'd hacked my computer or something.

"Your number? The school directory. Duh."

I wanted to sound angry, but I was too taken aback by everything, and I fell back on old, timid Kevin the Pushover. "What's wrong?"

"Is Aimi there with you?"

"Aimi? No. Why?"

"But you were with her last night."

"How do you know that?" Did he know everything about me?

Snowman snorted. "You made a huge impact at some monster party in the city. Some distant friends of mine said they saw you and Aimi there together, and that you put Troy back in the hospital."

Had I detected a note of approval in his voice? It was impossible to tell. I mean, this was Snowman, and he could sound pissed doing a standup comedy routine. "We wound up in the drunk tank at the police station, not the hospital," I corrected him. "Troy went home with his Gramma, but you might check the hospitals tomorrow. Or maybe the morgues. Gramma wasn't happy."

"Cool," he said with approval. "Did you take her home? I've been calling her all morning, but she's not picking up."

I watched some dirty newspapers flutter by. "I think she's kind of grounded."

"Kind of?"

"Majorly. Horribly. Eternally grounded. Her dad looked a little pathological last night."

"Mura...that old bastard." There was another pause, then Snowman said, "Why does it sound like you're sitting in the middle of some weird, post-apocalyptic movie?"

"Because I am sitting in what sounds like the middle of some weird, post-apocalyptic movie. I'm sitting on the corner of Jerome and Ocean Avenue and there's nobody around."

"You're out in the city alone?"

"Yeah. I guess."

"Why are you out in the city alone? Don't you know the military are moving in?"

I stared at my feet. "I don't know."

He sounded beyond exasperated. Obviously, I was the village idiot. "Look, she's not picking up at any of her numbers—and I think her dad's off chasing that fucking monster. I thought maybe she was with you. I've been calling around to all her friends, but none of them have seen her since yesterday."

"Well, she's not with me," I said as a bad feeling suddenly came to replace the numbness I was experiencing. "I acted like a total ass. She probably hates me and never wants to see me ever again. Hell, I don't want to see me ever again." I suddenly recalled the dream I'd had in blazing Technicolor, all the little details. The woman in the kimono plunging her long claw-like nails into Aimi's heart, and Aimi's eyes flying open in surprise.

I stood up slowly, wobbly, and said, my voice a faint whisper, "Does Aimi wear contacts?"

"Huh?"

"Does she wear contact lenses?" I repeated urgently.

"What does that have to do with anyth—?"

"Does she or doesn't she?"

"A lot of kids wear contacts. Jesus!" He sounded, as usual, on the verge of a conniption fit.

I, on the other hand, was feeling a lot worse than that. Aimi, like me, had blue eyes, but I was only now realizing it. Like me, she had found an effective way of disguising them, one so good even I hadn't noticed.

"Aimi's in serious trouble, isn't she?" Snowman said.

"Maybe." I glanced around foolishly, like there was transportation at arm's length. There were plenty of abandoned cars, but I was in the same boat as the looters. There was no way I was going to be able to navigate these streets, not with a car, and the buses weren't exactly running.

Then I spotted a used car/trade-in place across the street, selling everything from SUVs to dirt bikes, and I felt my spirits rise a little. "Where does she live?" I said, starting across the abandoned street.

For once, Snowman didn't sound like he wanted to rip my head off. He sounded scared. He told me as I stepped into the showroom. I looked over their selection of Hondas, spotting a very sweet looking Shadow with a candy-apple-red paint job and some serious muscle to it, but after checking the dealer's desks, I realized there were no keys to any of the vehicles. In fact, I had no idea where they kept the keys, but a good bet was a safe somewhere to keep them out of the hands of miscreants like myself. I swore violently and kicked at the panel of a hybrid. My heart was knocking somewhere up near my throat with panic. I had to get somewhere, and I had no way of doing it.

"What's going on? What's the matter?" Snowman demanded to know.

I glared determinedly at the Shadow. "I have to hotwire a bike, and I've never done that before." I transferred the phone to my neck while I uncased the hood, looking for the engine bay. If I could find the ignition coil...

"Smash the key ignition and find the rotation switch, stick a coin in and turn it," Snowman said, surprising me.

I hesitated. "You think that'll work?"

"I know it."

It was going to take too long to do this the right way. I ducked into the adjoining garage, found a good, heavy wrench, and carried it back with me. Even though the dealership was abandoned, I still felt a little guilty about smashing the ignition, which, true to what Snowman had said, revealed the key tumblers. I felt a cold, frantic energy bubble up through my stomach and into my throat as I inserted a quarter and twisted the mangled ignition switch. I had no idea if this was going to work, or if Snowman was putting me on.

"Yes." The Shadow roared to life.

I could have appreciated Snowman's advice—messy but effective—but I was far too frightened at the moment. I was almost certain I had killed the girl I was falling in love with.

9

I arrived at Aimi's building on Fifth Avenue in record time. It was a snobby, pedigree apartment building directly across from Central Park Zoo. According to Snowman, the Muras owned the penthouse triplex that formerly belonged to Laurence Rockefeller.

There was no doorman, thankfully. I think everything was running on a skeleton crew, if that.

Once I was inside the building, I was forced to slow down. The lobby was being manned by two very nervous-looking security guards watching KTV. Their purpose, I knew, was to keep the lowbrow riffraff like myself out, especially now, with looters hitting every part of the city. One stood up as I headed for the elevators. "Excuse me? Sir? You can't go up there…"

Oh yeah? Watch me.

I hit the call button as they moved out from behind the big, circular courtesy desk and started toward me. I was feeling frantic again. I had tried stabbing in 911 on the way over, but I kept getting busy signals. The city was officially swamped by calls, and the monster wasn't even here yet.

"Sir," repeated the younger of the two guards, the one that usually gets it in all the horror movies, "I'm afraid I can't allow you up there."

He was almost upon me when I turned around and extended my hand, palm up, which suddenly burst into a flamethrower. My hand tingled and then a jet of brilliant flames jumped from it and out at the guards, lighting up the face of the young one and reflecting in the glasses of the older one. A potted hibiscus tree caught on fire and started to burn merrily. The young guard stumbled to a halt and stood there in an apelike half-crouch, slack-jawed, staring at the tree crackling with flames. Maybe he'd seen the same movies I had?

"Get lost," I told him. "Go do something useful like dial 911. There's a girl in trouble upstairs."

The young guard said nothing, just hung there until the elevator car arrived. I backed up into it. Then the doors shushed closed and I was alone with the dull buzz of Muzak in my ears and my own dark thoughts rattling around my head. I couldn't help wondering if I was too late.

10

Aimi's big oaken penthouse doors were unlocked. I didn't know if that was a good omen or a bad one. The moment I pulled open one of the heavy, baroque doors, a slush of music papers slipped out and covered the floor at my feet. I didn't consider that a particularly good omen. I stepped over them and into the apartment, looking around at the massive, unfamiliar wainscoted walls, cathedral ceilings, and imported Pier 1-type furnishings.

"Aimi?" I said. My voice echoed. The penthouse was dark and silent.

I had an unnerving moment of déjà vu. I wasn't standing in a school corridor, looking for her, like in my dreams, but the echoing silence was still weirdly familiar and made the little hairs on the back of my neck stand at attention. No one answered. The penthouse seemed to be deserted.

The place was a wreck, like looters had been through it, yet nothing appeared to be missing—rather, the looters looked like they had been bent on destroying what was there. There were portraits and newspaper clippings behind glass on the walls, mostly of Dr. Mura getting this or that award for this or that humanitarian act, but the glass had been shattered by a blunt weapon and some of the portraits slashed. Furniture had been smashed to shards, and I saw a high-end chaise lounge with its intestinal stuffing hanging out, like a psycho with a knife had been at it. A line of ragged, half-crumpled music sheets covered the floor, leading me like breadcrumbs down a long corridor to a music room.

The room was huge, easily the size of my whole loft, but dim. There were reams of paper everywhere, covering the floor, the plastic-covered furniture, the ancient, preserved baby grand piano in one corner. The room would have been as dark as night, except that hundreds of flickering votive candles had been lit and covered every surface like a weird constellation of stars.

"Aimi?" I whispered again, my voice echoing uncertainty. I walked on the crumpled pages of the music she had once written, hundreds of pages covered in notations and black ink scribbles and scratch-out marks. She must have been blacking out her music for hours after she had come home.

A shadow flickered further on, in a dark recess. I turned toward it.

I'd finally found Aimi.

She'd tried to commit ritual Jigai—hara-kiri for girls. She had wedged herself between the baby grand piano and a desk and had tied her knees together with a long silk obi belt. I knew she had done so to bind herself into a dignified position in spite of any convulsions she might experience in death. On the floor beside her were more crumpled music sheets, and besides that a razor blade on a slim silver necklace, the edge of the blade covered in a shining thread of blood that looked black in the near dark.

"Aimi?" I said, kneeling down beside her. I was afraid to touch her. I stared dumbfounded at the blood seeping from dozens of gashes that covered her arms, her legs, her neck, even her cheeks. She had been cutting herself over and over, maybe for hours. What was worse, amidst all the fresh wounds were dozens of old white scars, hidden only because she wore so much clothing all the time. She looked lifeless, like a marble statue in black clothes, except that her chest was rising and falling fitfully. I pressed two fingers to her throat and found a thready pulse beating like moth wings against my fingertips, but her eyes wouldn't open at all.

"Aimi," I said again, surprised by how calm my voice sounded, even though a blade of panic was slowly cutting me wide open. I took her face in both hands, rubbing my thumbs against her cold, stony cheeks. "Aimi, it's Kevin. Aimi, open your eyes."

She made a low groaning noise like someone waking up—or trying to. With effort, she turned her head and her eyes cracked open—they were gummed together by the blood leaking from the tiny wounds all over her face. Her eyes were bright pale silvery blue, the color of the heavens after a rainstorm. I definitely understood why she wore the contacts. In her pale, Asian face, they looked surreal, almost otherworldly. My mind flashed over to a (perhaps) imaginary memory, a gawky, preteen Aimi being pushed and laughed at on the playground, and fighting back because she knew she was different. "Ke-evin?" she said.

"Yeah."

"Are we dead?"

"No, Aimi. We're not dead."

"Oh," she said, a painful noise.

"What did you do, Aimi?"

"Kevin," she said again, more forcefully. Her voice was dry and husky like she had been screaming for hours. She squeezed her fists closed so that more blood wept thickly from the wounds on her wrists. Despite all the blood loss, she didn't seem to be dying of it. Yet. Her eyes were huge and dark, the pupils almost completely dilated. She stared off into space. "We had fun. At the party."

"Yeah, we did."

"I didn't want to fight you. I...you..."

"I know you're a Keeper," I said to spare her a long, stuttering explanation. " I know you know I am too." The sad truth was, I had only just recently figured it out. *So much for a genius IQ*, I thought bitterly. "I know you're connected to Qilin."

She turned her head away as if she were ashamed of herself. *She won't last*, I thought, *not the way she's bleeding out from her wounds*. Though, from the sight of the blood surrounding her, I thought she should have been dead hours ago. Maybe, I thought, Qilin was such a huge part of her now that it wouldn't even let her die normally anymore.

Of course, I couldn't know that for certain.

That weird calm suffused me again, the same as when I had called Raiju forth that first time. I picked up the razor blade—it was genuine, and as sharp as sin—and cut the silk binding her legs. I ripped the fabric in half so I had two makeshift bandages of equal length and started binding her arms where her wounds were the most severe, pulling the silk tight against the deep black gashes in her wrists. It was the best tourniquet I could make in a pinch.

I picked up my cell phone and tried to reach 911 again.

"Don't," she managed, suddenly becoming animate. She shook her head sadly, her sweat-dampened black hair rattling around her pale face. "Please, Kevin, don't call the police..."

"I'm calling for an ambulance," I told her.

"Please...!" she cried. Her face contorted with horror. "I don't want them knowing...!"

"I won't tell them about Qilin, I promise."

She closed her eyes again. She looked exhausted, finished.

Miracle of miracles, I was able to get through. The dispatcher told me to stay on the line, that an ambulance was on its way. She started saying other things to keep me talking, but I turned the speaker off.

"It'll be all right," I told Aimi. "They're on their way."

She shifted uncomfortably until she was leaning against me. Obviously, her wounds pained her, even if they did seem incapable of killing her. "Don't tell anyone," she pleaded, panting through the pain. "Don't tell them about me. Don't tell them what Daddy did…please…"

I looked at the gashes, at all the blood. "What did your dad do?" I said, taking her gently and cradling her against me.

I thought of those eyeless MIBs at the police station. Dr. Mura had more than a vested interest in Qilin, I figured. He wasn't just interested in cleaning up after the monster. He was also trying to clean up after Aimi. It was no wonder he wanted me nowhere near his daughter. He was terrified my Kami would hurt Aimi. "He knows you're a Keeper, doesn't he? He knows about me too." It was the first time I had ever said the word aloud. I didn't like the sound of it. It made everything too real, somehow, too…final.

"Oh, Kevin," she said, "there's so much you don't understand. Just promise me you won't tell anyone about Qilin."

I saw the absolute horror in her face, but I could understand it. Something about being a freak makes you want to protect other freaks, even if they are your sworn, mortal enemies.

I held her. I took her hand and watched it curl slowly about mine, but her grip was weak and her eyes drowsing. Around us the candles flickered, the room full of flitting, moth-like shadows. I had to keep her talking. If she talked, she wouldn't slip into shock. "What did he do to you…and to Qilin?" I said, hoping the ambulance would hurry.

She let out a hitching breath. She started to cry, and the tears that leaked from the corners of her eyes were as black as the weird alien blood that had leaked from Qilin during the battle. They left shining, tarlike tracks down her cheek as they fell to the floor and burned holes in her music pages. "We made a mistake, Kevin, me and Daddy," she said. "A horrible mistake." She stared up at me with her bleeding black eyes. Then, slowly, she told me the rest of her story.

11

All of my life I've experienced horrible nightmares. Daddy took me to medical institutes all over the world, but none of the doctors could help me because there was nothing physically wrong with me. Finally, he started taking me to dozens of psychiatrists, but they, too, couldn't find anything wrong. He finally became so desperate that he started taking me to priests.

It was there, at a Shinto shrine at the foot of Mount Fuji that we learned about the Watchers and the Keepers. It was there that my Watcher taught me to summon Qilin, who is a water god. You wouldn't know it to see him now, but he was once a beautiful white serpent who guarded an undersea kingdom. I guess you find that very hard to believe.

My dad was not a very religious man, but he was very understanding, very open-minded about these things, and he worried about me constantly. He also felt that this was a good discovery—a breakthrough of sorts. His company had been struggling to clean up toxic spills for years, even though we weren't a very large or important company. Now, finally, he thought he could change that. He thought it might be possible to use Qilin to eliminate pollutants in the water. That way, something like Karkadon might never be born again.

I often played with Qilin in the water—he was very funny, and tame, and he would do whatever tricks I taught him to do. He was my friend, Kevin, my only friend, growing up. One day, Daddy asked me if I could train him to swallow toxic spills. He would do anything I asked, so of course he did that too. After a while, I trained him to listen to Daddy, to do whatever Daddy asked, and the company began to grow. No one knew, of course. It was our secret. We were so much in demand, especially after San Francisco that we were finally able to move the offices here, to New York City.

Then something happened to Qilin. He started getting bigger and bigger, doubling his size every day, and he was...changing. I guess he was becoming tainted from all the pollutants. He became...dark. He would no longer listen to Daddy, or even to me. He was eating too much, not just toxins and fish, but larger animals too. Daddy became afraid that when Qilin's food supply began to run out that he might try to come ashore. He tried to poison Qilin, to shoot him, all kinds of horrible things, but Qilin is a Kami, Kevin, a god, and the things Daddy tried to do to him only made him angrier.

I don't know. Maybe this is our curse. We have polluted the body of Amaterasu, and now we must pay a price for that. Daddy swore to me that after Karkadon, such a thing would never occur again. He wouldn't be responsible for creating yet more monsters.

He worked night and day to defeat Qilin—or, at least, to contain him. Qilin can't be contained, or stopped. He's not some manmade creature, Kevin. He's not a chemical spill, or some wild animal wrecking havoc. He's immortal, and he's different now. He no longer listens to me—or to anyone. He just wants to eat and to destroy. He's not the same Qilin anymore. Not my Qilin.

I love my Daddy, Kevin, and I'm so afraid. I wanted to stop him before he comes ashore again, before he hurts more people. I thought maybe if I died, the tether between us would be severed and Qilin would die as well, or at least go back to sleep like the other Kami. But it's too late now, and Qilin won't even let me die anymore.

12

"You didn't have to do this," I said, cradling her wrist where the blood was blackening her bandages.

Aimi's breath came in spurts against my chest. "I thought maybe without me, Qilin wouldn't survive, that he would go back to sleep..." She hesitated, taking a deep, shuddering breath, swallowing as if she were going to be sick. "The Shinto priests who taught me said a Kami cannot survive without his Keeper, one cannot live without the other, but...I don't know. I don't think Qilin will let me die. He's so strong now, so angry with me." She glanced up at me with glassy eyes. "I just know he wants to punish me, to destroy everything I care about. That's how vengeful the Kami can be. That is what happens when you betray a god."

I stared down at her, imagining her opening her flesh again and again to let this darkness out. The very thought of it made me feel sick to my stomach. I didn't know if I would have had the courage to do what she had done.

"I don't want to fight you," she insisted. "I don't want to fight your Kami. I don't want to fight anyone. I'm so tired, Kevin. So, so tired of everything." Every word pounded into me like a fist. She sniffed the black stuff pouring from her nose. "Do you hate me?"

I wiped away the black tears on her face. They left dark, grotesque smudges that gave her eyes a bruised and frightened look. "No, Aimi," I told her. "I don't hate you."

"But I killed them. The kids at the club." She started shaking like an epileptic. "They died because of me, Kevin, because I'm Qilin's Keeper..."

No, I thought. *Because of Qilin. And Raiju. Me.*

"It's okay," I said, even though I knew it was a lie. I knew nothing would ever be okay again. I held onto Aimi until I could hear the distant scream of approaching sirens.

13

I followed Aimi and the EMTs to St. Mary's on my bike. After they admitted Aimi to Emergency, they made me wait in the nearly empty patient's lounge where the TV was playing the Kaiju Network nonstop. I sat between a bruised, nervous girl who looked like a drug addict who was picking at scabs on her arms and legs, and an older lady who had a little boy who kept wandering off. An anchorwoman was reporting on more aftershocks being felt near the disaster zone as Qilin moved underground.

"...worse disaster this city has ever seen. Citizens are urged to stay inside their homes while authorities attempt to trap the monster within the sewer system. If you absolutely must travel, stay on major highways and be prepared for long delays, as thousands of New York citizens make their way to New Jersey and Pennsylvania in an attempt to escape further disaster." A cutaway showed the Lincoln Tunnel and the Delaware Water Gap corked with impatient traffic.

Immediately after the broadcast ended, the older woman got up with her little boy in hand and hurried for the doors. I felt my stomach do a back flip.

I thought about what Mr. Serizawa had said about the Kami, about how they would seek each other out in order to do battle.

109

What Aimi had said hadn't been any more reassuring. If she was right—and she probably was—Qilin might seek her father out, or me, just to punish her.

I sank back in my seat and covered my face with both hands and wondered what the hell I could do. I was stuck literally between two devils.

14

Around midnight they let me see Aimi in Recovery.

They had patched her up as best they could, but she looked very small in the big white bed—the bandages, the tubes going up her nose, the terrible machines. I approached her like some nightmare thing laid out in the laboratory of a mad scientist. Her arms were bandaged all the way up to the elbows, and I could hear her raspy breath through a respirator. She should be dead, but her bruised and tear-swollen eyes were open, watching me, her black hair spilling raggedly over the pillow around her. I sat down on the chair next to the bed and listened to the rhythm of the heart and BP monitor.

"Hi," I said, my voice hoarse. "How you feeling, beautiful?"

Her cloudy dark eyes blinked. "Not so good."

"Should I get a nurse?"

"I don't need a nurse." She struggled to sit up against the pillows, then started to pick at the bandages with her fingernails.

My heart leaped up. "Don't do that..."

"It's okay."

I winced as she started unwinding the bandages. I expected to see horrible black bruises and Frankenstein-like stitches decorating her arms up and down, but as the bandages came off, there was nothing to see. Aimi's arms were pale and unblemished, not even bruised.

I reached out and touched the smooth white flesh of her wrist as if to prove that the miracle was real. That it was true. Qilin wouldn't even let Aimi die properly.

I sat in that chair a long time, just holding her hand, looking at her. She looked tired, worn to the bone. More of that black stuff was leaking from the corners of her eyes. I reached for a tissue on the tray beside the hospital bed and handed it to her, watching her dab away the black slime. "I can't even cry anymore," she said. "Not the right way. Wouldn't you know, I kind of miss it?"

"What does it feel like?" I whispered, genuinely interested. "Being part of Qilin, I mean. Can you control him at all?"

She stared at me with hard eyes no longer blue; the black stuff had dyed them pitch black. "It's like trying to move in a nightmare when you're stuck. You know you have to, so you make yourself move. You control the nightmare. That's how I control Qilin...used to control Qilin, rather. Except...he's so angry, so big now." She shook her head slowly. "I betrayed him, Kevin. I can't expect him to listen to me anymore."

I waited.

She crumpled up the tissue, staring at the slime staining her hand. "You should know something else." She took a deep, shuddering breath and looked up warily into my eyes. "The part that attacked the club? It was only a little piece of Qilin. The larger part is still out there, looking for me, and I don't know if anything can stop him..." She stared down at her unscarred forearms as if she did not quite recognize her own body. "I wish I had died, Kevin. Maybe Qilin would have died too."

"You don't know that for sure," I said. "He might not die, even if you do. He is a god, after all."

She sniffed. "Are you mad at me?"

"Yeah," I said, and she looked up, surprised by my words. "Stop talking like you want to die. You didn't, so we have to think of something else." I sat silent a moment, listened to various doctors being paged over the PA system. "You could have told me, you know, if you knew what I was. I would have tried to help you."

She stared down at her hands and the little, chewed nubs of her fingernails. Her voice was so soft I had to strain to hear it. "I didn't want you to think I was a...a freak."

"Freaks of a feather flock together," I said and she jerked in surprise by my sudden humor. I lifted my hand, palm cupped, and imagined a small—very small—tongue of flame there. My hand shimmered and a candle-like flame danced up almost immediately. I felt a rush of adrenaline. There's something beautiful and very seductive about fire, which is why there are so many firebugs in the world. It can warm your soul, and destroy your life.

"You're a fire element," said Aimi.

"I can light my own cigarettes without a lighter. I make things explode when I get upset. I don't think I can be categorized as exactly normal at this point." I clenched my fist, snuffing out the flame before it set off the fire detectors in the room.

I couldn't understand why this was happening to us. It was like some big cosmic joke, and I was willing to bet there was a big, fat god somewhere sitting on his throne, giggling to himself— making Aimi like she was, and me like I was, then shoving us together in this city. All I could do was stare at her and tell the truth. "I don't care what you are. I don't care about the things you've done. Qilin was there at the club for me, not for you. This isn't your fault, Aimi."

"Kevin," she said patiently, sinking tiredly back against her pillows, "Qilin is looking for me, to punish me. That means anyone I'm around is in danger...look."

The duty nurse had turned up the TV in one corner of the ward. KTV was reporting on the earthquakes that were spiking steadily in the downtown area. Authorities believed it was Qilin on the move again and the National Guard had been brought in to help with evacuation procedures for Brooklyn and parts of the lower Bronx.

I couldn't help but wonder where my dad was, if he was okay. I hoped he would evacuate like everyone else. "Is it tracking you now?" I said.

She closed her eyes. "Yes, I think so."

"Isn't there any way to...break the link? Or block the connection?"

She shook her head, her tangled hair shushing around her pale face. "This is like a disease I'll have for the rest of my life, Kevin. I can control it, a little...put it in remission...but it won't go away, ever."

I stood up and paced around the ward. The nurse was busy with another patient and wasn't paying any attention to us. "Are you strong enough to walk?"

"I'm all right," she said, my brave Aimi.

I grabbed her clothes from a bag under the bed and tossed them down beside her. "Get dressed. We're getting out of here."

"Where are we going?"

"West, I think." I glanced up again at the TV. The shocks were steadily extending east, directly toward us, at about a mile or two an hour, despite the military effort. I knew they wouldn't be able to hold Qilin for long. He was a water god, and he could move through cracks, holes, sewer grates, anything, really. By my estimation, we had less than an hour before Qilin found us. We could use that time to ride west. If we were fast enough, and if the bike I had "borrowed" was good enough, we might be able to outrun Qilin. With any luck, we might even be able to land lock him. He was just sludge, after all, slime. If we could draw him away from any significant body of water long enough, we might be able to dry him out.

I told Aimi my idea while I watched the TV. It sounded crazy, even to me, but when I turned to gage her reaction, she was fully dressed in her flouncy black mourning dress and was slowly pulling on her boots. She sat on the edge of the bed, the laces untied, and dangled her legs off the side. "I don't think it will work," she said somberly. "Maybe we should just tell the military."

"Tell them what? That we have a couple of gods scoping each other out? That we can control them? Do you think they'd believe any of that?"

Aimi bit her lip. "What if we can't stay ahead of it? Or what if we can, but we lead it through a town or city?" She glanced up at me with her tired eyes full of shining black tears. "I don't want any more people to die, Kevin. I can't stand it!"

I went to her, knelt down and started tying her shoe laces for her. "We'll avoid the cities, stick to the deserted places, empty roads, ghost towns, forests. It'll be rough, but we can do it. We can lead it somewhere there's no water." I sounded so brave, so together, and my plan sounded reasonable. Didn't it?

So why did I feel like I had snakes freestyle jive dancing in my stomach?

She just sat there as if she didn't believe me. I half expected her to cry, but she was right. She didn't even have that anymore.

I took her other boot in my lap and laced it. "Don't worry. Once we're on the road, I'll figure out something."

"You're amazing. Like a white knight."

"Kevin the white knight," I said, and harrumphed. "I think you should know something. I used to be fat, and I play World of Warcraft constantly, and I picked my nose, and I even had a bug collection when I was nine. What do you think about that?"

She laughed.

I looked up. I didn't feel much like laughing, though I did smile, for her sake.

"What if it catches up with us?" she said, suddenly growing serious.

"I don't know, I'll think of something. One thing at a time."

She bowed her head. "I don't want you to die, Kevin," she said. "I couldn't stand that."

I stood up, pulling her up with me, holding her by the shoulders. She felt so light, almost birdlike. Breakable in my arms. "I'm tougher than I look," I said, hoping I believed my own bullshit. "A lot tougher."

"Yeah," she said, and hugged me, "I know."

15

We waited until the duty nurse was called out of Recovery on an emergency, then made a break for it. Downstairs, I brought the bike around while Aimi waited at the curb outside the hospital, dressed in my shades and jacket. I'd told her that I didn't want the overworked EMT teams coming and going to recognize her. The truth was, I was more afraid that the doctor who had worked on Aimi might have reported her arrival to her father. If Mura showed up, I wouldn't know what to do.

The moment I braked in front of the curb Aimi jumped on the back of the bike.

"Ready?" I said.

"I guess so," she said nervously, glancing over her shoulder like she expected Qilin to tear up through the street at any moment to catch us.

I let up on the brake and started to cruise out into the street. "Is it coming?" I said, feeling a dull electric shock of panic starting somewhere in my brain and zigzagging raggedly down my spine. Please, God, great Kami, whatever, I prayed, don't let it come…just help me out here a little…

"I don't think so," she said worriedly, "I just…"

"I know." I bit my lip. "Hang on." I swerved around traffic, which was already virtually gridlocked with buses and cars mass-migrating out of the city, all of them blaring their horns in a collective cacophony of noise that was difficult even to talk above without screaming. I took a side street, heading west toward the Brooklyn Bridge. From there I figured we'd pick up Canal Street toward the Holland Tunnel.

A quarter mile from the bridge, my worst fears were realized as a long black limousine pulled out into the intersection ahead us, scattering traffic like a bully busting through a school hall full of geeks. I hit the brake, nearly rear-ending the Greyhound bus directly ahead of us.

"Kevin…!"

"I know," I said, feeling Aimi's arms tighten around my waist. "I see it."

The limousine spun to a stop. There was no question in my mind. I recognized the driver behind the bulletproof glass—or, rather, the type: it was one of those Dagger-eyed MIBs that might just as well be an assembly-line robot. Japanese, with suit and shades. The back door opened and Dr. Mura ducked out, dressed in a wrinkled raincoat, his scowling attention fixed on us.

I heard Aimi suck in her breath.

Considering what he had created, what he was capable of, I wasn't about to hang around and find out what he wanted with me—or with Aimi. "Hang on," I said, spinning the bike around in the road. Almost immediately, I saw a second black limo pull out of the lineup behind us. Dr. Mura and his MIBs had really thought this out. With cars on all sides, there was no place to run. We were completely surrounded.

16

They were fast.

Before Aimi and I had a chance to slide off the bike, three of Dr. Mura's men started closing in around us. One put his hand under his suit coat. Before I could even react, a cab driver who had been laying on his horn the whole time ducked out of his cab and started shouting at the men in the black suits. More MIBs were circling like vultures going in for the kill, and I had a sudden, very bad feeling in the pit of my stomach.

The man with his hand in his suit extended his arm. There was a large caliber gun in his hand, like in a spy movie, a Luger or Browning. I put myself between the MIB and Aimi, but Aimi wasn't the target.

It all happened fast, too fast. The gun coughed three times, shooting out both tires on my bike. Then the cab driver went down, his head blown apart like a melon. I heard the rapport echoing off the street and surrounding buildings, but it took me a second to realize what had happened. They had actually killed a man in front of me.

"Kevin..." Aimi cried, her fingers biting into my shoulder. "Kevin!" But I couldn't look away from the old man lying dead at my feet, his blood mingling with the dirty water and trash in the gutter. The reality of it really hadn't hit me until that moment— that these funny zombie-men in dark suits and glasses had guns. That they would actually kill me and take Aimi...

I guess a part of me figured it was a game, a movie where the hero always gets out alive. One look at the dead man at my feet told me otherwise.

The MIBs were on the move, shifting around us like shadows. The street took on a fuzzy, dreamlike glow, like I was moving in a nightmare. One of the MIBs came up behind us and snatched Aimi away from me. I turned to fight, but one of the other MIBs grabbed me and twisted my right arm behind my back. Another leaned into me and I felt his knuckles go all the way into my ribs. I heard an audible crunch and the breath blew out from between my gritted teeth. It wasn't like with Snowman or with Troy. These guys were professionals. It felt like my body was filled with cement. I went down hard on the gritty asphalt, vaguely aware of Aimi's screams as she was hauled back toward Dr. Mura's limo.

Despite the pain, or maybe in spite of it, I managed to roll over in the street so I was looking up at the sullen grey sky. Dr. Mura stood over me, a grim look on his face. The sun reflected off his glasses and made him look eyeless. "You again," he said. It wasn't a cheery, I'm-your-biggest-fan type of greeting. "I warned you, little boy," he said. "No more warnings."

I could feel the love, I really could.

Dr. Mura nodded to one of his subordinates: "Shoot him. Shoot the Keeper." His voice was cold and dead, like he was making a laundry list. I had always thought the whole shoot-the-boyfriend thing was a joke in the movies, yet a robot MIB moved into place and dutifully lifted his gun. I held stock-still and stared down the grim black barrel that seemed to mark my future—or lack thereof.

"No!" Flailing and kicking in her MIB's grip, Aimi suddenly grabbed his holstered gun right out of his shoulder rig. Her eyes running over with black tears, she raised it and pointed it at her own head, her finger tensing on the trigger. "Kevin has nothing to do with this, Daddy. Let him go!"

"Aimi." Dr. Mura turned to his daughter with genuine surprise. For the first time he looked strained and old. He actually looked and sounded almost human. "Aimi, what are you doing?"

But Aimi was having none of it. "Let Kevin go, Daddy. Let him go or I'll end it here." She breathed roughly through her unnatural tears, her eyes fixed on me. Her hand shook, yet her voice was dead calm.

"Aimi," said Dr. Mura, hovering uncertainly between the two of us. He raised his hands in supplication. "I'm trying to *help* you. Kevin is a Keeper..."

"So am I, Daddy. So am I."

"If he lives, Qilin will have to fight him. Be reasonable."

"I'm not the one being unreasonable!" she screamed. She clicked off the safety on the gun to show him she meant business. I had a feeling she'd probably grown up around guns, that she knew how to use them. You don't mess with a person who knows the intimate workings of a firearm. "Let him go or you'll never control Qilin. Or me. Ever."

Dr. Mura scrambled to face his uncertain collection of lackeys. He let out his breath in exasperation. "Let him go," he said, motioning his men back. "Now."

The circle of black suits around me slowly receded, but I didn't feel any better. I was too busy down on my knees, aching and watching Aimi. She breathed in, out, in, out, but never flinched, and she never took her eyes off of me. I had a very bad feeling about that.

When the MIBs were as far back as the bottleneck would allow, Dr. Mura took a step toward his daughter and put out his hand. The bad feeling edged up a notch. I tried to shout something to Dr. Mura, to warn him back, but Aimi meant what she had said, and she gave me no time.

Aimi was determined. She closed her eyes.

Then she pulled the trigger.

17

I watched Aimi fall back onto the street in a slow-motion *ballet de action*, like something that had been choreographed, and, in a way, I guess it had. In a way, Aimi probably always knew it would come down to this.

I stood frozen in place, watching Aimi, swimming in my own dreamlike world where bad things didn't really happen to good people. It was a place I wanted to stay in.

If there was any light or life in her eyes, I couldn't see it, even though I could make out every other little detail about her, the bootlace that had come undone, the shining, tearless black of her unseeing eyes, the tiny jewel of blood at the left corner of her mouth. In that moment, I saw everything as Aimi fell back crucified in the grit and carnage of the street.

The ground split around her almost as if a holy thing had fallen, and cracks zigzagged out in every direction. A low rumbling sang from deep within the earth, a sound that escalated into a roar that seemed to fill the concrete and steel valley between the tall buildings that surrounded up to deafening levels.

Dr. Mura stumbled back from his daughter's body as if he did not recognize it, his eyes going everywhere at once.

I was on my feet, though I didn't remember doing that. I wanted to take a step back myself, I wanted to run away, truth be told, but the cracks in the ground were surrounding us and quickly widening as sudden, lightning-fast black tendrils began snaking out. I watched, wide-eyed, as they wound their way across the ground, toward Aimi's body.

Qilin was here.

CHAPTER FIVE
Burnin' For You

1

I cringed as Qilin rose screaming over us.

I looked over at Dr. Mura, but he was frozen in place, eyes closed, lips moving in a silent prayer as Qilin's appendages burst from the cracks in the street and surrounded us all like a wildwoods gone berserk. *Qilin must have threaded himself through the entire sewer system,* I thought. He was *everywhere.*

Tendrils snaked across the broken asphalt of the street and began winding around Aimi's body as if to embalm it. The whole street shook under the maniacal screams of the monster, making me stumble drunkenly in the gutter as I watched her body. It was dragged relentlessly across the asphalt and absorbed into Qilin's black stinking self-substance.

The worst part was, there was absolutely nothing I could do. I couldn't fight something like that, and if I called Raiju, the two Kami would turn this city into a smoking warzone. So I shifted away from the cracks and the coiling snakes with massive, flytrap heads, hissing and seeking.

The daylight dimmed and nearly went out as the tangled tentacles arched over us. I heard the sudden screams of Dr. Mura's men, and the futile, coughing sounds of their guns, then the men's cries were truncated. The great black pod-like heads bloomed into teeth and appetite and began swallowing his men whole. Pushing past his subordinates being plucked up into the garden of hungry mouths like bits of ripe fruit, Dr. Mura made a break for one of the limos parked cattycorner to the gutter. He had just managed to rev the engine and hit the accelerator when the largest pod of all came smashing down atop the hood of the car, shattering all the windows.

I lurched, shuddering, at the sight.

Somewhere in the shining darkness that followed, I thought I heard Aimi scream, the sound merging with Qilin's subhuman shriek of victory.

2

There was no definite form to Qilin. He was like a giant inkblot, or an amoeba with blood red eyes punched into a vague, bulbous head, and a few random tentacles sticking out of different, pulsating parts of his body. He couldn't seem to decide what form he wanted to take, but I had a feeling that wouldn't last. He warbled at me, shaking and sloughing off more caustic fluid. Laughing at me. Teasing me.

I had to remind myself that this was a Kami. A god. A very pissed-off god, corrupted by a pretty horrible man, and now master-less. I couldn't really think of a better recipe for disaster than this.

Aimi, I though as tears blurred my vision.

On the pavement, lay the broken necklace and razorblade she had used to mutilate herself on so many occasions. I wondered if she was still alive, and, if so, how much control she had over Qilin since becoming one with her god. I wondered if it was even fair to hope she was alive.

I scrambled back a few more steps across the burning asphalt, finally hitting the grill of an overturned cab. I couldn't possibly outrun Qilin, and since Raiju was his mortal enemy, I figured talking this over was pretty much out of the question. With my eyes riveted to the red, burning eyes set in the misshapen head, I edged slowly behind the vehicle, using it as a shield as the monster towered over me.

Qilin jerked spastically like a puppet on strings. Its gurgling edged up a notch, becoming a full-bellied roar of rage and frustration. One of its tentacles darted out like a hand swatting a fly, and the cab was suddenly gone—simply flipped out of the way as if it were made of feathers. The vehicle flew a hundred feet in the air, turning end over end before crashing down in the middle of afternoon traffic.

I flinched, fully exposed now. Chaos was erupting on the street, cars plowing into one another and tangling like ropes made of metal as they screeched to a halt around the cab burning like a bonfire in the middle of the street. Some even slowed to ogle the gigantic monster filling the street. It laughed at them, its attention briefly diverted by the fiery destruction it had wrought.

A part of me wanted to stay, to try to help Aimi somehow, but good sense prevailed—I was probably more my dad's son than I suspected—and I made a break for it in that moment, taking off down the street. Qilin noticed, of course. He was just a little too obsessed with me not to. I heard a rumble as he started after me, and the whole street rocked like a boat.

I am never going to make it! I thought. I was running full tilt, scampering over debris, my lungs on fire, and still, I could feel the cold evil wave of the monster behind me, trying to wash over me, to take me. I had just reached an intersection when a black van careened into view, stripping its gears as the driver downshifted in a hurry. I didn't recognize it at first. I just darted to one side to avoid colliding with it, but it suddenly spun sideways, kicking asphalt up into my face.

The palms of my hands hit the passenger side door with a resounding thunk. Qilin roared at my back like a hurricane bearing down on me. I didn't think, and I wouldn't have cared if the driver was a traveling psychopath, I wrenched the door open.

Snowman sat on the driver's side, his eyes fixed on the monster looming behind me. I couldn't look. I didn't ask how or why, I didn't question this miracle at all. I just jumped in the van and pulled the door closed.

"Drive!" I shouted at him.

He sat stunned, his hands at ten and two on the steering wheel, eyes staring off into space as if he was still trying to digest the sight of Qilin, however brief it had been. His Adam's apple bobbed up and down once as he swallowed.

"Drive, dammit!" I said again, smacking him in the shoulder to wake him up.

Trembling, his right hand fell on the gearshift as he shifted from neutral into drive. *"Ssshit,"* he hissed. Then he drove like a bat out of hell.

3

I leaned forward in my seat and bent my head between my knees to catch my breath as we jounced along the debris-laded road. I felt sore in places I didn't even know I had, as if my whole body had been turned inside out. Just beyond the walls of the van, I could hear the world going to hell.

"What the fuck is that thing?" Snowman screamed.

I could tell he was on the verge of hysterics. Hell, I was halfway there myself.

When I could breathe again, I lolled back in my seat and peered out the rearview mirror. About a thousand feet behind us, Qilin was slowly reshaping itself into a giant, crude, humanlike form, swinging its massive head from side to side as it searched furtively for me, throwing off corrosive black spatters that sizzled on the asphalt and burned vehicles down to their axels. For the moment, at least, it looked like I had given him the slip.

"Qilin," I said after a moment. I heard sirens in the distance. Police, ambulances, fire trucks that could do nothing about the monster pacing around downtown Brooklyn. If anything, the cacophony seemed to aggravate the beast. It lifted its gigantic fists and screamed to the sky like a petulant child having a temper tantrum, then slammed those fists down into a nearby building, smashing it like a toy.

I flinched. As we drove, I saw chaos erupting everywhere. People were abandoning their vehicles in the street and taking off on foot, carrying children, pets and possessions, whatever they could take. We were too far from the center of activity to see anything now, but Snowman had a TV set up in the back of the van. As he drove, I squirmed into the backseat and flipped it on, changing the station with the remote until I found KTV. True to form, a reporter was on the action, recording it from a news chopper overhead. Qilin was kicking at a line of parked cars in frustration, sending them clanking over into the street. A gas tank went off, igniting another—and another. In seconds, a mushroom cloud of orange fire burst heavenward like a bomb.

I gaped at the tidal wave of flames eating into the street and consuming the overturned vehicles. I felt like I was witnessing the end of the world. A fog of black smoke consumed the whole block, and I wondered what I could do...what anyone could do. If Aimi didn't take back control, we would all die, the city buried under millions of pounds of cooling black cinders.

We rode in silence for maybe ten minutes when Snowman finally pulled into an abandoned underground parking garage. We were somewhere in Midtown, the business district, by my estimation. I slid open the van door slowly, and immediately spotted Michelle and Rex waiting for us. That surprised me more than a little. Michelle had a seriously cool bike with her—her sporty new VTX Interceptor, the one I had helped her upgrade— but for the moment, I was too shaken to appreciate much of anything.

I tried to say something as I climbed out of the van, but my voice stuck in my throat for a moment. Finally, I managed to get out, "What are all you doing here?" Except that it came out sounding like a drunken moan, like I was in pain.

The driver's side door slammed shut. "Saving your ass, obviously," Snowman growled. It was good to know he wasn't panicking anymore and was back in Kevin-kicking mode. I think. Even out of makeup, dressed in a normal college hoodie and blue jeans, he managed to look and sound like a punk, and he pissed me off. He swaggered toward me, his eyes keen. "What in hell is going on?" he said, throwing his hands up. "And where's Aimi?"

"That *was* Aimi," I said.

He looked, as usual, like he wanted to slap me.

Before I could elaborate, Rex climbed into the backseat of the van, his bulk pushing me aside, his eyes fixed on the TV. "Oh man, this is so not cool, man," he said nervously. Under his patch jacket he was wearing a *Jurassic Park* T-shirt with the iconic Rex emblazoned on the front. Its jaws jiggled up and down as he trembled. I had created a monster, obviously. "Shell, Mamma and Daddy are so going to have a cow, and it's all Snow's fault."

"Nobody said you had to come along, chubs," Snowman said, and Rex gave him a puckered-out look, like he had a dinner plate in his lower lip.

My head was swimming. I wondered if I would pass out, if that wouldn't be for the best. I slid down to the cold concrete, hoping the chill of the underground parking garage would prevent me from either blacking out or throwing up all over myself—I didn't need the embarrassment of either right then. Slowly, everyone gathered around me, which didn't help at all.

"Is he okay?" Michelle asked, leaning forward, her hands on her knees, sounding concerned.

"He'll be fine," Snowman answered.

Unfortunately, in that moment, my stomach decided to revolt and I heaved up the meager contents of my stomach...right over the feet of the person nearest to me, who just happened to be Snowman. Let me just say, I got his Doc Martens good.

"Jesus!" he barked, dancing back a step. "He's such a wimp!"

"He's not a wimp!" Michelle said, waving her arms at him dismissively. *"Baboso!"*

"You so didn't just call me a drooling idiot!"

Everyone started bickering while I threw up one more time just for good measure. Rex, at least, had the presence of mind to get me a paper towel. I wiped my mouth, interrupting them all by saying, "What are you guys doing here? Aren't you supposed to be running like everyone else?" I sounded more annoyed than I felt. Truth was, I don't know what I would have done if Snowman hadn't been there to pull my fat from the fire—literally.

No, that wasn't true. I know what would have happened. I would have made a very nice flame-broiled Kevin Burger.

Snowman dug into a pocket of his hoodie for some unfiltered smokes that I was pretty sure he was too underage to have. "Yeah, well, I'm not the running type," he said, pulling one out of a pack with his teeth. I think they were cloves, but just then, my mouth was watering. I would have smoked anything to get rid of the pukey taste in my mouth.

"How did you know where I was?"

"I followed the monster," Snowman said, and everyone gave him their undivided attention. He leaned back against a column and took a long drag on his cigarette, enjoying the spotlight, as usual. "My dad's a Sergeant Major in the U.S. Army," he said. "He can be a real asshole, but being an army brat gets me all kinds of bennies, believe me."

"Like hotwiring cars?" I said.

He gave me his patented brusque-and-annoyed look. If he could have packaged it and sold it, he'd have been a millionaire overnight, believe me. "I've been using my dad's scanner to track Qilin. I've had to since you dumped me on the phone." His eyes burned accusingly at me.

I shrugged, like, whatever.

"I knew wherever Qilin was I'd probably find Aimi...and you." He nodded at the others. "As for them, after I phoned around they decided they wanted to help find you. Apparently they like you or something." He rolled his eyes dramatically.

This was just a little too creepy for me. "You know about Aimi, don't you? You know what she is..." I looked around, afraid I had said too much and would come off as Kevin the Crazy Boy.

"A Keeper, yeah," Snowman said around the cigarette clamped in his teeth, trying to light it. "Aimi told me a long time ago. It was my secret to keep...at least, until you came along."

"What's a Keeper?" Michelle interrupted, getting me a bottle of water to wash my mouth out.

"I wasn't a Keeper before I met her. She made me one," I said.

Snowman gave a derisive snort. "Nobody *made* you a Keeper, hothead. It's not freakin' vampirism. The ofuda makes you a Keeper."

"Yeah, well, I didn't know that until after I met Aimi."

"What's ofuda?" Michelle said.

I thought about what Mr. Serizawa had said, about telling the secret to only those you trusted with your life. I glanced up at Snowman, trying to figure him out. "Aimi must really like you to have told you what she was."

"I told you—she's my best girlfriend. Aimi protected me from creeps like Troy when I first came to this school."

That bothered me more than a little, but I set my current feelings aside. "Did she tell you about me? About our Kami being at war?"

"What's a Kami?" Michelle demanded to know, getting annoyed now.

Snowman grimaced around the smoke. "Nah. I put that together on my own. Aimi figured it was up to you who you told."

I finally trusted myself not to fall down so I climbed, swaying, to my feet. I leaned against a cold stone wall just to be on the safe side. "It's funny. I thought you were the Keeper. I didn't even know it was Aimi until last night."

Snowman's pale frosty eyebrows bobbed up at that revelation. "You thought I was a Keeper. I thought you were a jerk. No...wait. You *are* a jerk."

"Hello?" said Michelle waving her hands in front of our faces. "*Atencion.* Information required over here. Could you break up your little love fest long enough to inform us poor mere mortals what the hell you two are talking about?"

"Is this like *WOW*?" Rex asked, looking interested.

I wished. I looked at Michelle and Rex, then at Snowman. I could hardly believe all three of them had managed to set aside their differences in order to organize this little rescue mission. Nobody at my last school had ever done anything like this for me, and I felt an unfamiliar sting in my nose and behind my eyes. I didn't even know how I felt about it all until I realized I was sucking back the snot in my nose.

Screw it, I thought. I was just tired.

I felt I couldn't lie after all they had done. They deserved to know the score.

Michelle seemed to sense the fission in the air. "What happened to Aimi?" she said. "Is she all right?"

"She's gone. It took her," I said. "Qilin took her." Michelle stared at me like I was insane. I glanced over at Snowman. He nodded, then shrugged as if to say go on. I figured if Aimi trusted Snowman with her worst possible secret, and if he approved of Michelle and Rex knowing, then the decision was already made.

I started telling them about Aimi, about MuraTech, and what Aimi was mixed up in—and, ultimately, what she was. It didn't take long, but there was a deep silence after I had finished.

"How do you know so much about this stuff?" Michelle said, looking both pale and piqued at the same time. "I mean, is it a Japanese thing?"

"It's a Keeper thing," I said. Taking a deep breath, I went on to tell them about the Keepers, and about the War of the Kami.

I wouldn't have blamed them at all if they wanted to bale on the crazy guy who thought a bunch of teen wizards could control gods, but they surprised me. After I finished, they just crouched there, staring at me with bemused but open faces. Nobody ran off screaming into the night the way I had expected they would.

Snowman lit a new cigarette. After a thoughtful few seconds of contemplation, he sighed, shooting clove smoke train-like out of his nose. "Do you think Aimi's dead?" he asked. "I mean, did Qilin kill her?"

I thought about the scream I had heard. "I don't know. I don't think so. I think if he killed her, he might die too. It's more like he's...keeping her."

He nodded thoughtfully at that. "Well, if she's alive, then there has to be a way we can help her. There has to be a way for her to take back control. That or this whole city is going to go the way of San Francisco, you know?"

"I know," I said, sinking down against the wall. "Believe me, I'm open for suggestions."

4

The four of us sat around in a semi-circle on the asphalt and smoked. I found out that no one in our little circle had parents who knew where they were, and that didn't make me feel any better. If someone got hurt—or worse, dead—you could add that to my already arm-length list of offenses. But no matter what I said, how I reasoned, how I warned, or even threatened them, nobody seemed motivated to run away.

The clove Snowman gave me tasted like the bottom of a shoe, but I was seriously jonesing for a smoke. I mean, it had been that kind of day. Meanwhile, Rex flicked open his trusty Netbook so we could catch the latest live KTV feed without needing to crowd into the van. Together we smoked and watched Qilin staggering around in an almost drunken circle in the middle of downtown Manhattan, kicking cars, slicking streets and buildings with its caustic black acid, confused by all the smoke that hung in the air like heavy wet veils.

"I wonder how long he'll take before he just leaves," I said.

"Give it enough time, man, he'll eventually have to go back to the water." Snowman frowned at me. "I can't believe Aimi thought you were smart or something."

"I'm having a bad day."

"Look up in the sky, it's Captain Obvious!"

I looked at him keenly. "What's that supposed to mean?"

"You look like crap," Snowman snapped, stabbing out his clove on the asphalt. "Not that that's anything new with you, the Goodwill fashion refugee."

"I don't look like crap," I said. I let out a cough, but it wasn't the clove doing it. Heavy grey smoke from various fires on the street was beginning to leak into the garage in choking tendrils. "At least I don't dress like freakin' David Bowie playing the Goblin King, and what kind of stage name is Snowman, anyway?"

"Guys, cut it," ordered Michelle, looking like she wanted to smack us both. "We're supposed to be figuring out how to help Aimi, remember?"

Snowman got up and moved deeper into the shadows of the garage.

Michelle sighed. "I think you hurt his feelings with the Bowie comment."

I swore and got up. This was about the last thing I needed right now—Snowman and his fragile musician's ego having a hissy fit.

When I caught up with him, he was halfway across the parking garage, standing in the shadows, his back to me, lighting a fresh cigarette. Before I could say anything, he said, "I'm really worried about Aimi." He sounded like he might burst into tears. He took a deep breath and let it out before saying, "This is it. This is all real, and we're all going to die tonight, aren't we?"

It took me a moment to speak. "Yeah, it's real," I said softly, "but you're not going to die, and neither is Aimi." I sighed and leaned against the wall beside him. "Look, I know you and Aimi are close. I'm really happy about that. Seriously." Slowly, I let out my breath. I felt an enormous burden melt off my shoulders. I was giving up, giving in. "I won't mess up what you guys have together—whatever it is."

I listened to the silence ticking between us. I felt like I owed him that, at least, for saving my ass—even if he was a huge jerk. "I'll bring her back. I promise." I sounded more confident and knight-erranty than I felt in that moment. Actually, I was feeling pretty shitty. I was going to bring the handsome hero and beautiful heroine together, and wind up alone in the end. Story of my life.

Snowman's linebacker shoulders lifted and fell. "Ah...fuck it," he said, like he had come to some decision. He turned around and threw down the cigarette. I thought he was going to punch me again and instinctively balled my fists up at my sides, readying myself for the assault, but instead, he set both hands on the wall to either side of me. Then he leaned in and looped an arm around my neck and steadied me as his mouth came down hard on mine, and I mean hard, like he was ravenous. I reached up to clench his shoulders, to detach him from me, but he was way stronger than I had anticipated and I wound up just hanging there, stuck between the wall and his body, as he kissed me, his tongue sliding effortlessly into my mouth.

A lot of stuff suddenly made a lot more sense to me in that moment, particularly Snowman's relationship with Aimi—and with me. Snowman and Aimi weren't the hero and heroine of this little tale, and they weren't going to wind up together. That was the good news. The bad news was, I had been a kissing virgin until now, until Snowman.

Sure, I'd had a bunch of dates back in San Francisco, but always with the fat outcast girls, and always, it seemed, at the local library. Believe me, nothing very interesting had ever happened between the stacks. I had never even made it to first base with a girl—though I had secretly hoped that Aimi would change all that for me.

Was I ever wrong...

Snowman could have done about a million things to me in that moment, things that I could have handled. This I couldn't handle. After some breathy moments that reminded me of those embarrassing scenes in movies where the hero and heroine are doing some serious tonsil diving, and you're stuck watching it sitting beside your parents, he finally let go, and I fell back against

130

the wall. He stared at me so fiercely I felt like he was x-raying me with his eyes. "Sorry," he whispered. He sounded hoarse, not sorry at all, and way more breathless than I was comfortable with. "I mean...we could die tonight, and if we do...well, I wanted to know what it was like with you...oh, you know."

"Um..." I said, my patented response to all things that baffled me to the soul, "Okay." It's hard to get angry with a guy who's that worked up. Plus, Snowman is a really good kisser, just in the event you ever end up dating him.

I really, really wished I hadn't just written that.

Snowman eyed me, not with malice for a change, but with curiosity, as if he were waiting for a reaction from me. I didn't know what to say, and I sure as hell didn't know how to react, so he ruffled my hair in a brotherly way, then stood back and casually lit a new smoke, like nothing had happened. "There has to be something we can do. Some way we can help Aimi."

I stood there, slumped against the wall, doing my best to recover from everything. I didn't even know where to begin. Between the sirens and police ban and the choppers passing overhead, the evacuation in full swing, it sounded like the end of the world was going on outside. All I could do was stand here, listening to it all, helpless and useless, and realize I had just had my kissing-cherry popped for the first time in my life.

By a *guy*.

Snowman wasn't the least bit embarrassed, of course. He just stood there, pale and icy, looking at me expectantly, waiting for me to have some revelation as to how to help Aimi, his best girlfriend. A typical performer, I suppose.

Then it hit me. I didn't think I could help her at this point, but maybe Snowman could.

5

I told the others my idea in detail.

I started out thinking it was a terrific plan, but as I went on, self doubt started to nibble around the edges of my self-confidence and soon I was worried that it was all useless, a fantastic waste of breath. Finally, I just stopped speaking and stared down at the chewed nubs of my fingernails and the clove burning fitfully between my first and second finger. The others were utterly quiet like they didn't know what to make of it. Not a good sign. I expected Snowman to be the first to shoot me down, so imagine my surprise when I glanced up and saw him staring long and hard at me like he thought it might actually work.

"Some crazy shit," he said at last. "Do you think you're up for it?"

"Yeah," I said, "I could do it." Not knowing if I could do it at all. "I think if she really heard you—you and your music—I think she might have a chance to take back control of her Kami. At least, I hope so." I looked around at the faces watching me, totally out of ideas.

Snowman scratched the back of his neck. "What if she's not...you know...alive anymore? I mean..."

"Then we did whatever we could."

"What about your Kami?"

"Oh, hell no." There was no way I was going to summon Raiju unless I absolutely had no other choice. Anyway, I had kind of skimmed over that part of my story.

Snowman considered that. "I have the equipment." He indicated the van parked in the shadows. "I mean, I could do it, but I don't know if I could get the decibels out, even with good sound equipment. I never sang for a monster before."

"Don't you have amps or something? The equipment you used in the club?"

"Um," said Snowman doubtfully. "It's a club, Kevin. We use a few second-hand Fenders, but we don't have gear for outside concerts. In fact, I doubt an outside concert will ever happen at this point. We're not exactly slated for Central Park next week, you know." He said it as bitterly as possible.

"Maybe we could broadcast it?" Michelle suggested. She shrugged.

"On what?" snapped Snowman.

"Radio? TV?" Michelle shot back, showing her teeth. "How about a billboard or something? Use your head, *baboso*."

I thought they would start fighting again but Rex butted in. "How about the Astrovision?" He looked up from his Netbook, nodding his head like he was grooving on music only he could hear. As usual, he was virtually unaware of the fact that the city was falling apart around us. The Internet was still running, so all was well with the world. "It's like the biggest billboard in the city, man. I don't think Qilin could ignore that."

Snowman bit his lip. "That's in Times Square. Isn't KTV broadcasting from there?"

"I could take that signal, man."

"Excuse me?" I looked at Rex. Maybe he really could rewire a bike, and hack some school computers, but to pirate a whole TV station...?

Rex gave me an evil grin. "Child's play, man. Back in 1977, a guy in Syracuse took over Channel 7 and broadcasted episodes of Star Trek by using a guitar amplifier. Same principal, just everything's easier these days, because it's all digital." His eyes held a dangerous sparkle. I had definitely created a monster.

"That's great, Terry, but we'd still have to lure it to Times Square," said Michelle, staring at the smoke filtering into our little HQ and twisting around us. I could feel the distant thrum of footsteps as the monster stomped its way through Midtown. "I mean, it's not going to do us a favor and just check out the Astrovision 'cause we said so."

"I'll take care of that," I said immediately, standing up. "It's looking for me anyway."

Snowman raised his eyebrows. "I don't think so," he said. "No. Absolutely freakin' not. Do you think you can outride that thing?"

I gave him a hard look. He sticks his tongue in my mouth—which, by the way, I was still reeling from—and suddenly he's calling the shots?

I. Don't. Think. So.

I crushed out the clove and jammed my hands into the pockets of my jacket so no one would see them shaking, and realized I was scared half to death. "If Rexman can jam the KTV transmission, I sure as hell can outride a monster." I turned to Michelle. "That's if Michelle will let me borrow her bike."

6

Unlike Jennie, and the Shadow I had borrowed, the VTX Interceptor was built for sport and high maneuverability—and looked it, too, with a super-light aluminum chassis and an updated fuel-injected V-8 engine. A track machine, built for razor speed. Alignment or no, I could still cut a hundred times better on it than on the Shadow—which, by the way, was probably buried under a ton of rubble.

Michelle looked her over with pride. "She's fast. Cuts like she has a mind of her own. Do you think you can handle her?"

"No problem." I had helped upgrade her. A week ago, I would have been drooling over the handlebars, completely oblivious to the rest of the world turning around me. Right now, though, the only thing I cared about was whether it would go fast. I felt a dull, trembling sensation under my feet that I didn't have any desire to stand there and contemplate. The hackles on the back of my neck were telling me it was nothing friendly, nothing good.

Qilin was seriously on the move again, searching for me.

I mounted the bike to get a feel for her. It felt sleek and space-age. I kicked the engine over, listening to her roar to life, then tested the brakes, front and back. Everything checked out, so I turned the engine off and started walking her to the edge of the parking garage, peering out at the blackening sky.

I felt like I was doing a very stupid thing—mostly because I was. This time I was not only smacking the wasps' nest and not running away, I was actually sticking my butt in the air, inviting it to be stung. Taking a deep breath, I threw a leg over the bike, wincing as all my sore spots protested the action.

Before I could kick the engine over, everyone started gathering around me. Michelle was first to offer me a grim smile and say, "Good luck," like I was riding out to battle, never to return. It didn't instill a lot of confidence in me, but I tried on a nervous smile anyway. If I was going to die horribly by doing the bravest, stupidest thing I'd ever done in my whole life, I wasn't going to go out all gloomy and Gothic.

"Thanks," I said.

Snowman pushed to the front of the group. He looked piqued in the cheeks, like he was trying fitfully to find something to say. Finally, he reached out and took the frames of my sunglasses in his hands and pulled them off. I stiffened, blinking in the bright light I was so unused to. Everyone was surprised by the sight of my naked eyes—it was the first time most of them were seeing them—but no one made any comment. Michelle smiled, leaned forward, and kissed me on the cheek, while Snowman clutched my glasses and stared at me, lost, afraid.

I looked around at the gathered faces of my crew, the pinched, worried, young expressions. The kid expressions. That was the worst thing of all—I was reminded that we were nothing but a bunch of kids doing this, trying to do what the military could not.

I cleared my throat. "Does everyone know what to do?" I said.

Slowly, one by one, they looked at each other, then they looked at me and nodded.

"Anyone want out?"

Again, they looked at each other, but no one spoke up.

"You're nuts, you know that?" Snowman complained.

"I love you too, Snow," I said, throwing him a kiss. Then I was off.

7

The VTX rode like a dream.

I watched big military jeeps tearing up the streets on both sides of me on their way to fighting the big bad monster. The scream of artillery shells bursting in air filled the far distance, and the air was so full of smoke it was as black as midnight, even though it was only a little after noon, according to the Interceptor's built-in digital clock.

I had taken the most dangerous job. The suicide run.

But you knew I would, didn't you?

I swerved around a gridlock of thirty or so cars stuck at an intersection. All of them were trying in vain to escape via the Brooklyn Bridge, which looked like it was plugged with so many military personnel that it was impossible for anyone to get off Manhattan Island at this point. I popped the bike up onto the sidewalk, then took an alley, hoping to cut out the main roads. By my estimation, my crew would reach Times Square in about ten minutes—assuming they didn't run into problems along the way, of course. Deep in my heart, I sincerely hoped that stupid army brat would bring Michelle and Rex through okay and with no injuries. I certainly didn't need that on my conscience along with everything else.

Qilin was busy tearing into the Trump Tower when I arrived. He had mutated again and looked more like a giant, black, multi-armed octopus than anything else, though those keen, crimson eyes remained. He wasn't happy. Pretty obvious, what with the trees he was uprooting and the asphalt he was cracking in huge flaking pieces by pounding against it with his tentacles like a kid having a temper tantrum. *Just great*, I thought. I had to aggravate the most pissed-off god in the history of humankind.

Qilin turned his glistening red eyes on me the moment I stopped in the street in front of him. He stopped with a huge tree in one upraised tentacle. He looked confused by my appearance. I guess he wasn't expecting me to come to him.

I was alone, no military backup: the road was too badly torn up for even the heartiest Humvee to get this close. Anyway, the army teaches its soldiers not to stupidly run toward monsters, but away from them. Me, on the other hand...I leaned over and picked up a piece of mortar the size of a softball. I put a good wind-up on it and hurtled it directly at one of those ginormous rolling eyes.

Bullseye!

Qilin screamed, tearing up the street as his tentacles flailed in response.

"Yeah," I said, "your mother."

I jerked the bike around and hit the gas, narrowly avoiding the tree as it slammed into the ground inches behind the bike. I checked the rearview mirrors. Sure enough, Qilin was on the move, a mass of crawling chaos pursing me, tearing up shards of stony asphalt and throwing them at me like a pissed-off kid. Using my mirrors, I swerved right and left to avoid the falling debris like I was riding a giant slalom. Up ahead, a manhole cover was blown skyward, looking like an oversized penny. I saw more of those squirming Venus flytraps lurching upward out of the hole—*My god*, I thought, *the thing must be rooted in every inch of the city's sewers*—the jaws clacking together in hungry anticipation.

I jerked the Interceptor to one side, riding the sidewalk around the looming, snapping appendage, then gave her the gas full-on when I hit the street again. It might kill her, but at the moment, I was more worried about being eaten alive than the bike burning up under me. The Interceptor coughed and there was a scary, heart-lurching second when I feared I had done her in, but she kept up her speed in the end, like she knew this was her shining hero moment.

Behind me came that ominous thunder underground as the monster took to the sewers after me, and the distinctive snapping sound of asphalt as it was smashed from the underside of the road as if with a series of angry, pummeling fists. Grit rained down on me and caught in my hair. More manholes blew as I rode past them, with still more tendrils crawling out, as if Qilin had stretched himself to cover most of lower Manhattan.

As I neared an intersection, I heard a tremendous roar that made the whole street shake, a sound that left me deaf for a moment and aching in my bones. A car fell trashed in the gutter inches away, looking like a twisted up soda can. I jerked the Interceptor around it. Something swept by overhead like a giant flyswatter and smashed into a bus lying on its side in the road, pulverizing it to flying shards that spilled out into the street in front of me. I used what looked like a very flattened car in the road ahead of me as an impromptu ramp to get up over the debris, saying a little prayer to Evel Knievel as my tires left the road. It was great hang-time, but in my current state of absolute terror, I found I couldn't appreciate the maneuver at all.

The moment I landed on the other side, I gave the Interceptor all the gas I could, riding faster than I had ever ridden in my life, certain that at any moment, I would feel those tentacles closing around me, then teeth taking away the light...

Something brushed the back of my neck. I heard Qilin's hackle-raising scream, almost human—like a child, denied. The sound made my teeth hurt and my bones vibrate, but I rode on. I rode to outride the reach of the monster.

The bike began to cough again, but I didn't let up on the acceleration and I didn't stop shaking with adrenaline until I was several blocks away.

8

I made one pit stop on Broadway. I grabbed my cell, but there was no service. I jumped off the bike and picked up the receiver of a pay phone outside a minute mart, hoping to get through to my dad, to tell him how sorry I was about everything, in case I never saw him again, but the lines were dead. Even the most primitive forms of communication had been obliterated in the crisis.

I stared at the receiver as if trying to project my thoughts down the dead wire to him.

Next door, a television was running in the broken picture window of a used furniture store that had been abandoned and vandalized. A KTV anchorwoman was talking about armed forces moving into Manhattan to combat Qilin. Meanwhile, the President had declared a national state of emergency and was discussing the use of military-grade weapons on Qilin.

I dropped the dead receiver and watched the camera cut to live footage of convoys on the move back on Fifth Avenue—trucks, military jeeps, and a confiscated snow plow that was sweeping dead vehicles out of the way for the troops to pass on foot. Soldiers in camo and combat uniforms were shooting at Qilin with high-powered military rifles, but their ammo passed harmlessly through the slimy thing and just blew chunks off the surrounding buildings.

Qilin writhed in the street, snapping those Venus flytrap heads at anything that moved within ten feet of it. The camera jittered around to take in the full breadth of the monster—a giant mass of darkness easily the size of the school I had attended before my life went to hell and didn't come back. Qilin recoiled from the barrage of firepower being unloaded into him, but it was a mere reflexive action; no projectile could cause him any real damage. He lashed out at the soldiers, his red eyes roving contemptuously over the puny little men trying to stop him with their useless, spitball-like bullets.

Qilin's whip-like tentacles swept vehicles and soldiers aside, sending them flying into the air like little toys. He made his jolly laughing sound again, a sadistic noise like blades rubbing together, then spattered the whole area with thick black shining ink that burned corrosively through the bodies of trucks and cars in the street. A building began to crumble as Qilin used his tentacles to pull it down atop the soldier's heads and vehicles.

When the clouds of dust and debris finally cleared, I saw the skirmish line—what was left of it—retreating, and military tanks and armored jeeps moving to fill the place left empty by the ineffectual soldiers. Giant combat cannons mounted atop tanks and jeeps fired noisily at the monster undulating in the middle of the street, generating his shining sea of black sludge and industrial waste and lashing out at anything that moved.

I wondered if Snowman, Michelle, and Rex had made it to Times Square. We had to end this, and we had to end it now.

The President flashed onto the screen, looking sleepless and severe, and started delivering a public address while flashbulbs went off in his face and White House attendants ran back and forth frantically in front of the camera. It was a recap from earlier in the day, according to the ticker at the bottom of the screen. He started talking about the possible use of nuclear weapons to destroy the creature that was, even now, destroying downtown Manhattan.

Nuclear weapons. But Qilin was made of nuclear waste. I had no idea what a nuke would mutate him into, but I had a feeling it would be nothing good.

I stared at the useless receiver hanging dead on its umbilicus. Numb, I rushed back to the bike.

9

So there I was, Mr. Nobody.

I had to stop a monster, the military, and the President of the United States from turning the country into a nuclear wasteland. And I had to do it by slaying a god, and, quite possibly, by killing the girl I loved.

And you think you have problems.

10

The cloud of smoke and ashes was getting worse with every passing mile, almost chokingly thick, making everything as impenetrable as midnight. I flicked on the bike's high beams to cut the gloom.

I was missing the sun at this point, but as I sped through Midtown, I realized there was an advantage to the dark. I could see lights up ahead—Coca-Cola and Virgin signs flashing as we neared the epicenter of the United States. I was almost there. Everything looked intact and KTV was broadcasting live over the Panasonic Astrovision, one of the city's largest spectaculars, giving people vital information for evacuating the city. Best of all, the Destroyer van was parked lengthwise across 42nd Street, near the subway. I pulled the bike to the curbside, but I didn't have to kill the ignition. She made a croaking noise and gave up the ghost under me with a belch of smoke. I dropped the bike ingloriously to the asphalt and raced around to the back of the van.

The van doors were open and Rex and Michelle were sitting in the back. Michelle was holding an impressive-looking DV-rig camera, while Rex cradled a Netbook that was in the middle of doing a complex operation. He threw me a walkie.

"You made it!" Michelle cried, swinging the camera around so it was pointed at the center of Times Square.

"Did you do it?" I asked Rex, clipping the walkie to the belt of my jeans. I was panting breathlessly and felt like I was going to fall over from a heart attack. "Is it hacked? Tell me it's hacked."

He pointed the way Michelle was filming. "Check it."

I turned to face the two-hundred-foot-tall Astrovision, the biggest one in Times Square. KTV had confiscated both it and the news crawlers earlier in the week. In fact, they had been controlling them for days, ever since Qilin's existence had been confirmed. As I watched, numb and almost swaying with exhaustion, the gigantic vision of a concerned anchorman grew snowy and began to break up into tiny digital pixels. The little pieces began blinking out one by one, until the screen had gone completely black, cutting off the reporter in mid-speech.

I held my breath and waited, staring at the despondently blank screen.

A few tense seconds passed, then the screen came up again, this time featuring a gigantic, animated Tyrannosaurus Rex bobbing up and down in a ferocious pose. It let out a terrific roar before vanishing off the screen, only to be replaced with Michelle's jiggle-footage of Time Square with a ticker running along the bottom of the screen that read REX-TV FILMING LIVE FROM TIMES SQUARE.

Rex grinned, giving me two thumbs up. I was pretty sure whoever was in charge of the feeds for the KTV news teams was scratching his head right about now and wondering why he no longer had control over the Astrovision. Unfortunately, mingled with my relief was a feeling of pure, unrelenting horror, and somewhere, in the back of my mind, I was trying to calculate how many years' jail time we were racking up by pirating a major news station.

Onscreen, Snowman was standing in the center of Times Square, an acoustic guitar hanging from his shoulder. He looked small and nervous, nothing like himself. For one moment, I felt my confidence slip and I was reminded that we were four kids who didn't know what the hell we were doing. I didn't want to die. I didn't want my friends to die. Then Snowman glanced up and spotting me, he nodded. It was then that I remembered that we were also the only ones willing to do something other than bomb the city of New York into oblivion.

We didn't have much time. I picked up the walkie and told him to go. He nodded again and reached up to slide his earphones and mike into place. I turned back to the van and saw that Rex had boosted Michelle to the roof. She knelt there, trying to get a steady, in-frame shot of Snowman. Rex grabbed a pair of headphones and stuck one to his ear. He nodded to me to indicate the audio was working.

Down the street came the shuddering of a giant body moving underground. I could feel the vibration all up and down my spine, making me tremble with a dull and horrible dread.

Snowman took a deep, shuddering breath and closed his eyes. His fingers played over the guitar strings, a high, strong note. Then he began to sing. For Aimi.

11

The ground trembled, signifying Qilin's approach, but there was nothing to see, no monster topping the buildings crowding around us. It was going to be a subterranean attack. Qilin was a coward.

I turned to stare at the Astrovision. A two-hundred-foot-tall Snowman filled the screen. His eyes were closed and his lips were moving, but all the manhole covers in the street exploding at once and flying off into the distance drowned out the sound of his voice. Seconds later, the snapping black flytrap heads began emerging, undulating snakelike along the ground. Snowman stopped singing and just stood there, watching them writhe across the asphalt toward him. One of the flytraps snapped inches away from the toes of his boots. He swallowed and took a step back.

I thought he would run—I mean that would have been the sensible thing to do—but it turned out he was almost as crazy as I was. Ignoring the slithering mutations writhing and hissing around his feet, he closed his eyes and began to sing, first faintly, then louder, stronger, as he started to find his groove. Mind you, his was the gravelly voice of a singer used to belting out metal lyrics. No real grace required, but as his voice rang out over Times Square, he put enormous emotion into it, molding the words as if he were singing them for the first time.

Do you remember the red sun we shared
With your crying face, we bid forever a goodbye
I watched you dance in those waves of yesterday
I wrote your name in the sand and outlined it in shells
All broken
And then the waves took it all away
But the red sun remained and we shared that last goodbye
Forever
I close my eyes and remember a beach of broken shells
Do you remember the red sun we shared
When my heart broke that first time
Forever

Snowman stopped strumming the guitar and looked up at all the flytraps that were hovering and hissing overhead like a many-headed hydra, watching the Astrovision. There were tears in his eyes and a quiver of absolute fear in his playing hand as it jangled over the strings of the guitar. The hydra heads were slowly braiding themselves together, their black Jell-O-like bodies merging into a giant armored black serpent that swayed uncertainly in the street, its hooded, beadlike eyes fastened to the screen as if it was being hypnotized by a Kamir snake charmer.

I thought about what Aimi had said about Qilin, the snow-white water serpent, and I wondered, briefly, what he had looked like before Dr. Mura had tainted him. I wondered if it was anything like this.

Snowman swallowed at the awesome sight of the Kami pulsing before him, bigger than ever before, so big it eclipsed the lights. His breath hitched and he stumbled back a step. "Aimi?" he said, his voice booming out over Times Square as well as the rest of the world. "Aimi...are you there?"

Qilin let out a long rattling hiss like a hydraulic machine turning over and began writhing in the intersection, its powerful musculature knocking over cars and buses as it twisted and writhed in the street. For one heartbeat, I thought Snowman had done it. That the music had been enough to restore some part of Aimi's will, and that she was fighting to reclaim control of her Kami. Then the serpent tilted back its scaly head and began to scream to the heavens like it was in mortal anguish.

I knew what was going to happen seconds before it did. I darted out into the street and tackled Snowman like a semi-pro QB, the two of us smashing into the door of the storefront just under the eaves of the Astrovision. A second later, the serpent drove its head like a massive battering ram straight into the Astrovision above us. The roar of the explosion was deafening. I pressed Snowman back, pulling up my leather jacket to try and cloak us both. I watched in the glass of the storefront as a waterfall of razor-sharp LED glass smashed down into the street, shards pinging off the sidewalk and unzipping the back of my jacket as they bounced off.

I could hardly breathe, but I didn't lower my jacket until I realized how close I was to Snowman, and we were more or less in each other's arms. I lurched back, crunching glass underfoot. That was way closer than I wanted to get to His Esteemed Gothicness.

What a mess. Glass was scattered everywhere, and it was a miracle that we hadn't been ripped in half. Ozone was thickly choking the air, the smoke of the Astrovision only adding to the darkness already blotting out the afternoon sun. Everything looked like midnight…in a pit of Dante's infamous Hell.

I sighed tiredly and shrugged off some glass shards.

Snowman looked dazed, a gash above his eyebrow leaking blood into his eye. He touched it, winced, then slid down the locked doors of the storefront until he was slumped on the stoop, staring at his feet.

The walkie on my belt squawked. I picked it up as I tried to peer through the haze.

"What the hell happened?" came Michelle's near-hysterical voice.

"It didn't work," I said. My voice sounded hollow and weary, old beyond measure.

"No duh."

"I want you and Rex to get out of there now."

"But…"

"*Now*, Michelle. I'm not fucking kidding."

Snowman was glancing around at the debris, his shaking hands fumbling in his pockets for a smoke. He shook his head, his eyes slowly widening at the breathy, hellish noises that Qilin was making out there in the smoke. "Jesus…it's going to kill us. I mean, we're really going to die here today." He looked up at me unexpectedly. "I don't expect we could…you know…" He crossed his first and second fingers.

"No," I said immediately.

He lit the smoke and leaned back against the door. "Wow. Anger management issues and a raging homophobe."

"Shut up." I took the smoke from him and dragged on it like it might be my last. Under the circumstances, it probably was.

In the glass of the storefront, I spied my eyes. They looked paler than ever, liked fired steel. Old. I shrugged and the jacket fell off me in a half dozen pieces, just so many strips of black leather, singed and battered.

Clenching the cigarette between my teeth, I extended my hand and concentrated on summoning the cold Kami fire. I was so overwrought, it was no trouble at all. It erupted right on cue, like it was waiting for me. Within the tall column of blue flames, I grasped the hilt of the sword.

"Cool," said Snowman.

Somehow, it didn't feel that way. This sword was our last line of defense, and the only way we would ever survive this—the only way the city would survive this. I narrowed my eyes at the sound of Qilin screaming in the smoke and hell that pressed in on all sides of us. Soon, it would return to finish the job—destroy us, then destroy the rest of the city as Aimi lost all control over it. The reasonable part of my mind told me to grab the bike and ride, but that wasn't a solution, only a temporary fix, and if I ran, Qilin would just continue to pursue me, wrecking everything in its path and killing thousands as it grew bigger and bigger. It might get so big it blanketed the entire face of the planet in a sea of burning black slime.

Kevin the White Knight, I thought. The clove burned up in my hand. I gasped the sword with two hands and stepped out into the street to meet my enemy head on. Through the swirls of sulfuric smoke, I caught glimpses of the modern advertisement surrounding me—the lights and colors, the promise of continued humanity and growing technology—and took my ancient burning sword, the ofuda that could call a god, and raised it high over my head. I glanced over at Snowman, sitting there huddled in the doorway, surrounded by glass and destruction, waiting expectedly for some miracle to save us all.

I had no miracles. The best I could come up with was me.

I took a deep breath and said, my voice groggy and sad with resignation, "Hey, man, enjoy the show." Already I could feel the power coming to me. Think of the best you've ever felt in your life—the first track and field you'd ever won, the first time you landed the leading part in the school play, your first kiss—now take that times a thousand. I felt like I could do anything, that I was indestructible. It was a very seductive feeling. I closed my eyes and let the sword guide me up and down as I carved the sacred kanji into the air before me.

I thought, *Raiju...come...come now!* and drove the sword resoundingly into the ground at my feet. I stepped back and waited.

I felt the familiar vibration, the terrible fecundity of life beneath my feet. My hands began to sweat around the hilt of the burning sword. With a belching roar of fire and a wave of hellish heat that left me dizzy, Raiju reformed before me, its claws raking the ground with streaks of fire. Before it was even fully formed, it tilted its head back and bellowed to the heavens. Then it planted its burning claws on the street and stared down at me with an almost human face and flaming, holy blue eyes that reminded me strangely of the woman in my dreams. The woman in the red silk kimono whose hair was on fire.

She.

It hit me like a gut-punch. *She.* Raiju was *female.*

Raiju snarled, the sound like a storm in my face, and bared her teeth, each easily the size of the sword wedged in the ground between my feet. I smelled fire and blood on her breath. But the teeth didn't frighten me, not the way the eyes could, the way they pierced through layers of my flesh, unearthing every desire, every mystery, every secret within me, peeling my soul-skin back to expose myself to the Kami's second sight.

I looked back at her. I felt tired and old and small and afraid. *My darkest secret,* I thought, *there you have it, my lady: I'm afraid. I'm a sixteen-year-old kid and I'm afraid I'm going to die today.* "And if you want to kill me for that," I whispered, "get on with it already."

She opened her mouth—it was as large around as a cavern—and an enormous black tongue unfurled, raining saliva down. I saw flames cooking within her mouth. She grunted and the black tongue flicked over me. It was like being covered in a huge, hot wet blanket. The impact drove me to my knees, but I still managed to hang onto the sword.

"Just do it!" I screamed, feeling nothing at last.

The tongue retreated inside the fire-lined jaws instead. She snorted sulfur and seemed to smile. *I think not,* she said in her hissing, sensuous voice. *Not yet, handsome.*

"Don't call me that!" I screamed at her, meaning it. Aimi had called me that, and Raiju had no right to it.

She grinned at me, enjoying my pain.

"Do as I say."

She halved her burning eyes at me in challenge as she padded around me, almost soundless on her feet, seething and stinking of anger and sulfur. *Why should I do that?*

A flicker of self-doubt licked at the back of my mind. I had control over Raiju, I held her leash, but it wasn't absolute, and we both knew that. Aimi had betrayed her Kami and had lost all control over him. I could easily end up the same way. A big part of me wanted to beg and plead with her, tell her I would do anything she wanted if she would just let me live. Another part of me knew that that was the wrong way to handle a god. If she cowed me, she would know I was weak, and then she would be the master.

I was not weak.

"Because I am the master," I said, reassuring my grip on the sword, ready to pull it from the ground at a moment's hesitation and send her back to hell.

Say it.

"I am the Keeper!" I screamed.

Raiju laughed like she had achieved a victory and sank back into the swirls of hellish smoke to wait.

12

The funny thing about death is, you never see it coming until it's staring you in the face. Until you're forced to look it straight in its burning red eyes. You go about your life worrying about your always-late homework, you're I'll-never-get-the-nerve-to-ask-her-out, you're I'm-so-gonna-fail-class-big-time, thinking it's the end of the world. At least, that's how I always approached things.

Until today. Until I found myself standing in the trembling rubble that had once been New York City, the sky inky black and choked with dust and debris, the neon lights of Times Square struggling fitfully to pierce the almost impenetrable darkness, the air full of that rotten-egg stench of open gas mains that I hated so much, and realized I was going to die today.

I watched the kaiju rise before me, through the passage of a torn-open manhole cover. It seemed to go on forever. Black against the black sky. Then it curled over—centipede-like, though it no longer resembled that—and stared at me with brilliant crimson eyes. It looked at me, and it looked through me, this thing that wanted to kill me, this thing that wanted me dead.

Dead, because I stood between it and the rest of humanity.

Me. Mr. Nobody.

A big part of me wanted to rage against whatever gods had conspired to bring me to this, to end my life so callously, but I had a feeling it would do no good. I had a feeling I had always been destined to be here today, to die like this.

"Aimi," I said to the thing, softly, quietly, wondering if it understood me, or if my words were nothing more than unintelligible gibberish to the creature hovering before me, clomping its jaws with anger and hunger. "I know you're in there somewhere. If you let this thing happen, you'll never forgive yourself. Remember the kids at the club?"

The asphalt exploded into shards that rained down dust and debris around me as Qilin's tentacles ripped through the street. Gradually, it reformed itself yet again. It looked more reptilian now, with a long face that ended in a mouth that was split almost from one eye to the other, and filled with jagged yellow teeth. It tilted its head back to the smoky sky and screamed, black slime-like tears running off its face in burning rivulets. It seemed to be in a state of constant flux, changing back and forth between humanoid, plant, and animal, as it filled Times Square, its body a twisting canvas of ever-changing life forms, except for those eyes, those hideous red eyes that always remained the same.

It was still screaming in pain and horror as a nest of twenty-foot-long spiraling horns—black and shining and as sharp as bone—suddenly sprouted from between its eyes. It reared over me, and I felt its freezing-cold shadow descend as it drove its killing horn at me.

I snapped my eyes closed. I raised my hands in self-defense and cried out in the last moments before the kaiju lashed out at me. I couldn't face my end this way, I just couldn't, Keeper or not.

But nothing happened. Nothing at all.

I opened my eyes to a wash of red heat. Raiju was standing over me, staring at Qilin with pitiless human eyes, her claws clenched about the horn that would have pierced me right through the center of my body had it been allowed to descend even a foot more. Her eyes narrowed and burned an angry blue like twin butane flames. I felt a sickening wave of fear roil through me as I stared at the black horn suspended mere inches from my head.

I was afraid, yes, afraid Raiju might not save me in the end. But I harbored a greater fear—that she would, and she would tear through any enemy to do so, with or without my approval. In this case, however, I had given it to her. I gave it to her when I declared myself her master. I had given any enemy—including Aimi—over to her, as she had undoubtedly wanted me to, and by doing so, I had proven myself worthy of her.

I thought again of the dream, of Raiju piercing Aimi through the heart with her claws. The realization made me so sad and sick I wanted to die.

Raiju's massive jaws dropped open, smoke drifting from between her massive teeth. It took me a moment to realize that it was her smile, a sadistic sight. *Raiju likes you, Master*, she said. *You will go far, Master. You will be mine.* Gripping the horn, she used her enormous strength to flip the monster over in the street.

With a roar, Qilin crashed back into the Times Square Building—through the building—making the street shake with the impact. Chunks of glass and steel exploded outward, crashing past me like meteors striking the earth. One piece ripped the center part of the street up like old carpet so the running railways beneath were exposed like toy trains.

I felt the earth lurch and gripped the sword for purchase to keep from falling through the hole and into the subway below. A massive shard of a billboard sign slammed into the street in front of me. I stared, sweating, at it, disbelieving my luck. Vibrating with strangely unfelt fear, I steadied myself, then turned my attention on the two monsters grappling in the debris of the Times Square Building. They rolled over, snorting imperiously at one another, and the final battle began.

13

Raiju was a dirty fighter, I'd give her that. She fought the way I fought, putting everything she had into it, exploiting any weakness she could find in her opponent. No honorable combat.

No need for it, because this was all about survival, and anyway, I doubted there was any honor among monsters.

Raiju grappled with Qilin as the thing's many-tentacle arms wrapped themselves securely around Raiju's neck. Qilin screamed as he encountered her burning mane, but made no attempt to release his foe. In response, Raiju grasped the snapping, pod-like head of one of the tentacles trying to strangle her and ripped the jaws apart until they foamed and fell open like the broken petals of a withered flower, then tore it entirely from the stalk. The rest of the tentacle went slack and dropped to the street far below.

Qilin, larger than ever before, twice as large as Raiju, and more distinct in its form—a more upright prehistoric form, with a snapping, gator-like head and those long horns quivering from the center of his misshapen skull—sent out dozens of sludgy black tentacles that whipped wildly around Raiju's neck in a stranglehold. Raiju thrashed and struggled in Qilin's grip, but each time, she managed to pry off a tentacle, two more appeared to take its place. There was no way she could untangle herself from Qilin's grip.

Qilin laughed at her struggles, his toothy grin splitting his face nearly in half in a nightmarish way. Then he turned and started slithering his way out of Midtown and toward the Hudson River, where he undoubtedly planned to take refuge in its polluted waters—and where Raiju's flames would be effectively snuffed out. He dragged Raiju ingloriously behind, raking her through broken streets and half-demolished buildings; the rubble giving off sparks of light and fire, the tentacles tightening into ever-tighter, noose-like knots around her neck with each passing second.

I started to cough. I could feel Raiju's once enormous strength ebbing away as Qilin began literally to choke the life out of her. The flames along Raiju's body slowly dimmed, going out one by one. I felt her thrashing, once-powerful body weaken. I coughed again, feeling the terrible constriction at my own throat. I could feel the pressure cutting right into my breathing—I could feel what Raiju was feeling as she began to die. I dropped to my knees as the street seesawed dangerously in front of my eyes.

Raiju raised a forepaw in defense, but Qilin only laughed his snide, gurgling laugh, and lashed out with another tentacle, driving it like a spear through Raiju's palm and into her throat. Raiju gagged, bloody black foam seeping out the corners of her massive jaws. *Master*, she said, her voice growing weak in my head. *Master, help me…*

I rocked forward, clutching my throat, coughing bloody droplets onto the broken ground. Mr. Serizawa had said nothing about taking damage for your Kami. There was simply no air left to breathe and my lungs felt like they were full of concrete. I ripped at my shirt as darkness began seeping into the corners of my eyes. For a horrible moment, I gave into an overwhelming feeling of defeat. Years ago, I'd been helpless against bullies like Bryce. I certainly hadn't had the power to save San Francisco, or even my mom, for that matter. I really wasn't much of a hero, whatever Aimi thought. Hell, I wasn't even much of a son, of late.

The flames of the sword glowed bright neon blue. I set my jaw and gripped the sword in both hands. I could do absolutely nothing about the past. I could only do my best about the now. That was all I had, and as the sound of Raiju's cries grew fainter in my mind, little more than a whisper of breath. I directed my terror and my loss and my loneliness down, feeding it into the ground with a cry and a massive burst of fire. I directed it into the Kami under my control.

Raiju let loose a ferocious roar that sounded like it was being ripped from the very center of her being. Finally, she clutched the tentacle stuck in her throat with her claws, and even though she was drowning on her own blood, even though she was in terrible pain, she managed to rip the whole tentacle from Qilin's body in a gush of foul black fluid that slicked the streets and surrounding buildings. She screamed as she pulled the tentacle from her own throat, and I could feel the sound razoring my brain open, but I refused to release my hold on the sword.

The ragged wound in her preternatural flesh burned with fitful blue fire, knitting itself closed in seconds. Oxygen flowed back into her lungs—and into mine.

Rising with a reverberating snarl, Raiju climbed to her upright, bipedal position, her lips curling back over her saber teeth, and began lashing out at the tentacles that bound her with renewed rage. The fire along her mane and back leaped higher, burning not red this time, but cold blue, like her eyes, like the fire that now danced along the blade of the sword and up the backs of my hands, surrounding me in a burning blue halo. She did the smile-thing, her mouth falling fully open, but this time a blast of brilliant blue fire burst from her enormous, slavering jaws, a fire so hot it engulfed the front of Qilin's whole body in seconds and made the beast's tentacles explode into fountains of burning black fluid.

Qilin screamed, staggering stiffly back like a creature gone blind with pain, his clawed hands scraping blindly at the open air full of burning debris. Raiju narrowed her eyes as she took a moment to admire her handiwork. Then she suddenly charged in for the kill. The two kaiju clung together in a death lock, but even now, with Raiju at full power and Qilin wounded, Raiju found it nearly impossible to kill the beast. Each time she grappled with an arm or a tentacle, the black atomic sludge slipped between her claws. Try as she might, she could not get a handhold on Qilin, as malleable as water and as caustic as hydrochloric acid, and the more she snatched at the toxic flesh, the more her clawed hands burned, and the more Qilin shifted away.

Soon, Qilin would retreat, slipping down the deepest holes into the city's underbelly to reform, to wait, to strike elsewhere. Raiju would have to finish off the monster within the next few minutes, or risk losing it forever.

14

A military convoy was headed my way, cresting the rise in the street. A line of vehicles followed. Times Square would be swarming with soldiers in minutes, but I didn't have minutes. We didn't have minutes. Soon, Qilin would slip away, and the military would be powerless to stop it.

I turned my attention back on the battle taking place in the burning rubble of a half dozen buildings. Raiju, in desperation, had resorted to her most primitive weapons and was lashing out at her enemy with her enormous claws, ripping chunks of the creature away in boiling streaks of fire as she dug into him, and through his tough outer hide into his soft, toxic innards. Qilin screamed and tried desperately to retreat, but Raiju had him by the insides now. I winced each time she pulled at the rotting poison mass within the creature and flung parts of it away, filling the street with steaming piles of offal.

Aimi, I thought, feeling numb and almost delirious with pain and horror, she was most certainly dead by now. In fact, I hoped for it. For Aimi to be alive and suffering within that monster...

Raiju roared and finally drove her fist right through the thing, withdrawing it so quickly an enormous pile of festering muck was torn loose from the heart and flew two hundred feet in the air, slamming down into the street at my feet, spattering both my jeans and the sword with inky, toxic black sludge. The wounded Qilin staggered back, weaving with pain and weariness, a hole through his heart, or where his heart would have been, had he had one.

The two monsters eyed each other warily.

I held my breath, waiting, watching Raiju finger the burning black slime between her claws. With a frustrated bellow of pure rage, she slashed at the air in front of her nearly formless enemy, then suddenly leaped on Qilin, slamming the full weight of her bulk against the nearly eviscerated monster. Qilin flew backward into one of the few remaining standing brownstones, the whole structure crumbling down atop him and pinning him soundly under a million pounds of burning bricks and rubble.

Qilin made a last attempt to reform into something smaller, something that could slip away, but Raiju opened her massive jaws and let loose with another blast of blue fire like a flamethrower on high.

Qilin, at last, began to burn.

He tilted its head skyward and let loose a shrill scream of torment unlike anything I had heard him emit up until now, the very fabric of his being breaking apart, his eyes bursting like balloons full of rotten water. Pieces of his body broke away as the fire pouring from Raiju's jaws consumed him and blew those pieces heavenward in burning black clouds that stank of death and disease and every manmade disaster.

Raiju finally closed her jaws and blinked slowly at the remains of the creature.

Qilin's claws flailed uselessly and his head twisted from side to side, but from the waist down, he was simply...gone. And still he fought on, mindlessly trying to rise, to run away.

Raiju leaned over the creature to examine him. Qilin suddenly thrust his head upward, and the longest of his horns penetrated Raiju under the jaw with a searing pain that I felt all the way to my brain. Raiju screamed as she grasped the horn between her long, black claws. With a mighty wrench, she yanked the horn from the top of the monster's head, long strings of sludge sliding off Qilin's malformed head. Slowly, she pulled the horn from her own throat and held it in both hands as that, too, turned to black slime that ran through her fingers like muddied rain.

The pain made her mean. The pain wiped away any mercy she might have shown her fellow Kami.

She turned her attention on her enemy one last time. I felt the blue fire come to her—come to us both—and again my hands caught fire, burning so hot and cold at once that I screamed and clutched myself with the utter, mind-searing pain of it all. It was the deepest, darkest pain within me coming to horrible life, burning up, bursting forth. I felt my rage. I felt Raiju's own. Her eyes glowed bright, heavenly blue as a final burst of white flames coughed out from between her massive teeth. She poured that white-hot, smelting fire into her enemy, bathing Qilin up and down, burning him and the building rubble around him down to soft, crackling black stuff. Closing her jaws and smiling savagely, she punched at the monster's head, bursting Qilin into a mountain of flyblown pieces that crumbled away.

Her eyes blinked at her work with an almost human intelligence. Without making another sound, she turned away from the ruins and looked directly at me, and I heard her voice deep in the innermost whorls of my brain: *A gift for you, my handsome Master.*

She smiled at me. Then she roared savagely in the last second before I pulled the sword from the rubble and the fires of sleep consumed her and she was gone once more from this earth.

15

I had no idea what gift Raiju had given me, and to be honest, I was too exhausted and battle-weary to care.

The sword fell to the broken ground and burned up, and I followed soon after.

Lying there in the rubble, my hair and clothes smoking, I waited to vomit, but my stomach was painfully empty. I could only manage a few pathetic dry heaves as wisps of white smoke drifted off the surface of my skin. I was so tired I thought I might die right then and there. I almost wished I would.

All I could think was, *She's gone. Aimi's gone. I killed her. Oh God, I killed Aimi...*

The convoy was here at last. I could hear sirens and trucks crunching over gravel as they drew as close to the disaster zone as they could. I realized I wasn't going to pass out like I wanted to, and I really didn't want to be found here and taken back to the police station, so I pushed myself up, scrabbling amidst all the debris. That's when I spied movement out of the corner of my eye.

The great lump of black sludge that Raiju had torn from Qilin's heart was moving. My heart lurched, then seemed to stop dead in my chest. *Oh God*, I thought, *please don't let it be alive...not again.*

As I watched, the slime fell away and a thin, ragged girl stood up, covered from head to foot in shining black tar, her hair in greasy tatters plastered around her pale, drawn face. She shivered and hugged her shoulders, then fell to her knees in utter exhaustion.

"Kevin," Aimi gasped, "he's gone. Qilin's gone."

Raiju's gift coughed up some muck and then gave me a tired and sad smile of victory.

EPILOGUE
The End of the Beginning

1

The Hole was rebuilt six months later and dedicated to those students who had lost their lives. Around that time, I started seeing posters going up for the grand reopening all over the school halls. Aimi asked me to be there. She was playing for Destroyer in a gig that would be broadcast live all over the country and the internet simultaneously.

Michelle told me all the details while I worked on her bike.

I scooted back to show her how I had tightened the manifold on her VTX—I mean, I felt I owed it to her, since I had pretty much killed it. I pointed my pocket flashlight at different parts of the engine, explaining how each section worked together. It was a sweet bike, but the alignment was even worse now that I had mangled it.

Michelle had given me a new nickname: Kevin Takahashi: Slayer of Bikes. She also helped me upgrade Jennie as part of my Shop project. That way, she said, I wouldn't eat up any more of her own Shop projects. Rex had disengaged the killswitch, and Michelle had given Jennie a lighter frame and a fantastic new paint job—black, with flames and skulls. She said she was determined that Jennie should look kickass in case I ever had to do stupid, insane stuff again. Not that I planned to do stupid, insane stuff ever again. Promise.

That Saturday, the night of the big concert, I stood there in front of my closet door mirror, fixing my clothes and choosing my glasses. My dad poked his head cautiously into my room. He and I had been slowly bridging the rift between us, but it was slow going, a lot of work. He asked for less out of me, and I tried to do him more favors. Somehow, we met in the middle, even though neither one of us were talking much. The night he hit me remained between us, un-discussed, unobserved, but I preferred it that way—if we didn't discuss it, it didn't really happen. That's what I told myself, even though I knew it was the fattest of the big, fat lies.

"Do you need a lift to the club?" he asked, resting his shrunken bulk against the doorway. His eyes looked tired, his face darkened by beard because he had forgotten to shave again. His apron had plenty of grease stains, naturally.

I buttoned the cuffs of the black satin club shirt with embroidered sakura along the lapels that Snowman had lent me for the night. He said that way I wouldn't look like a Goodwill refugee anymore. He told me my hair was hopeless, though. "I'm good," I said, smoothing down my old broken-in blue jeans. "I want to take Jennie out, show off her new moves."

I waited for him to say something about that, about me being grounded or whatever, but he just stood there, silently watching me like he didn't recognize me at all. I looked at him in the dresser mirror. "I'll be back before midnight. Promise." I opened the top drawer of the dresser where I keep my glasses, opting for my little rosy Ozzies.

Dad continued to stare at me in the mirror, brushing at the silver just recently cropped up in his hair. He looked like he wanted to say something. Then he suddenly noticed the pack of Blacks in the open drawer atop my tee shirts. I blame Snowman, because he's the one who got me hooked on cloves. I waited for Dad to freak, to lay into me. Instead, he turned away. "Try to be back by midnight, okay?" he said, making no mention of the smokes.

I listened to his footsteps receding down the hall. I felt a pang. I thought about going downstairs, talking to him. Telling him…but tell him what? Mr. Serizawa was right. The less my dad knew, the better. The safer he was. I ran my hands over my face and hair, brushing it out of my eyes. I loved my dad, but I knew there was no easy, fairytale fix to our story. This was real, this was really happening to me, and, ultimately, I was alone.

I slipped on my riding jacket and fixed my glasses and brushed the wiry long hair off my shoulders. It was longer than it had been six months ago, and was still completely unmanageable, but no one made fun of me at school anymore. My crew wouldn't let them.

I started down the stairs, running into Mr. Serizawa along the way. "You look most handsome tonight, *Mago*," he said.

"Do you mean that?" I said. It didn't bother me so much, the things Mr. Serizawa said. There were a lot bigger things on my mind these days.

"Very much a...how do they say it in this country? A heartbreaker."

I grinned at that.

He looked at me. He looked through me, the way Raiju could. He said, rather suddenly, "But are you well, *Mago*?"

"I'm fine," I said with some hesitation. "I mean, it doesn't show, does it? The, uh, Keeper thing?"

He nodded approvingly. "You look quite normal."

"Thanks."

His look turned keen. "But are you all right? Are you well?"

"Well enough."

"And the other. How is she?"

I felt a stir within. I fingered the glasses. I didn't know what to say, and I barely understood what she was. "Sleeping," I said, "she's asleep."

"But she wakes in your dreams, yes?"

I thought of the red-haired woman, flames like flocks of birds on her kimono. Laughing at me. Smiling at me almost every night in my dreams, because in the end, I had done her will, despite being her Master. A deep worry had begun nibbling at me of late. Mr. Serizawa had said that some of the Kami were good and tame, and others evil and destructive, and that the good ones and evil ones would seek each other out to battle for control of earth. Aimi's Kami had been a good Kami, once, before Dr. Mura had tainted him. So what did that make Raiju?

I clenched my fists at my sides, determined not to think about it. "She won't wake again in this world, Mr. Serizawa," I told him. "I won't allow it. I promise."

"I hope," said Mr. Serizawa, "that the great Kami sleeps in peace from this day forward, and that you are able to keep your promise forever, *Mago*."

I told the truth. "Me too, Mr. Serizawa. Me too."

2

As I rode toward the club, I thought about how much New York had changed.

It didn't look like New York anymore. Maybe someplace in a war-torn part of the Middle East, or some other planet. Homeless caravans lined the streets, and relief aid stations were set up on every corner. Buildings were little more than blackened holes in the ground, their steel skeletons pointing crookedly at the heavens. The whole lay of the land had changed, and that was just property damage. Human tragedy had left an even bigger impact on the city. There wasn't a block that didn't have a dozen homeless people loitering around trashcan fires or soup kitchens, and massive carnival-size tents had been erected in every vacant lot in the city to house hundreds of homeless families as reconstruction carried on endlessly in the inner city. Hospitals and morgues were overflowing.

We had been lucky. Japantown had been spared much of the damage. The Red Panda was one of the few remaining restaurants in this part of the city and business had picked up considerably—so much so that Dad had reconsidered the move. That was a good thing. It meant that, at least, I wouldn't wake up in the morning surrounded by polar bears and penguins.

It was true. My life was starting to look up.

Qilin was dead, and the concert was being held as much in celebration of that as anything else. Everyone at school seemed to be at the club tonight, the parking lot so overfilled it was hard to find a parking space. Then I noticed Michelle and Rex standing next to Snowman's van, waving me over, the space between the van and the chain-link fence just wide enough for me to squeeze Jennie in.

"Kevin, man!" Rex cried, waving frantically to me and doing that weird little Tweedle Dee dance. "You're late!"

"Do you know what traffic is like in this town?" I said as I pulled in. "Especially now?"

"Snow was all over me. You were supposed to be here an hour ago." He adjusted the tuxedo jacket he was wearing over his geektacious I PUT THE STUD IN STUDY T-shirt. "Damn, man, I think he was crying."

Groan. I like Snowman. A lot, but he's still a pain in the ass, and if he ever pulls that kissing shit on me again, I will kill him.

I looked over at Michelle, who shrugged and rolled her eyes all at once. Despite it all, I was feeling very lucky in that moment. I had two great friends who were alive, who had made it, when so many others in this city had not.

Michelle looked hot. She had traded in her tomboy clothes for a red swing dress with little pink skulls embroidered along the hem, which was a major improvement on her former wardrobe, in my opinion. In fact, she had a hell of a figure when she chose to show it off. Her hair was tied up in a high Bobby-Sox-style ponytail, and her makeup was minimal but perfect, bringing out the amber specks in her brown eyes. She thumbed the back entrance. "You better go console the crybaby, hero."

"Ugh," I whined, bowing my head over the handlebars of the bike, "Do I hafta?"

"Yes, Kevin," she answered sternly, "you hafta."

3

Inside the club, techno beats were emanating frenetically from the opening act—twin girls, dressed in matching black diving suits, with cellophane dresses overtop. Kids were raving like crazy, and there were free exotic juice drinks at the bar to celebrate opening night.

I slipped between all the sweating, gyrating bodies, making my way backstage where the brand new dressing rooms were set up. I rapped on the door, sighing and thinking about how Snowman was going to pound my face when he found out I was late for his big gig. The door opened a crack and Morta peeked out, her spiraling red Raggedy Anne hair full of black ribbons and plastic black butterflies. "Hey, Kevin," she said, "you're late."

"I know." I stuck my hands in my pockets. "Is he pissed?"

"Scared, more like." Morta grinned, thinking it was very funny that I had to play nanny to His Gothic Highness. She stepped back to let me pass, lifting up the hem of her Bo Peep dress in its shimmering waves of black taffeta to keep it from dragging along the floor.

Inside the room Dust and Ashes, dressed in matching tuxedoes, were sitting on either end of the sofa, tuning the instruments. Morta ran back to them and started passing messages back and forth between the two brothers. Both guys refused to speak outright, even when called on in class, and they would only whisper things into Morta's ear, who then had to relay the messages. Mental roll of eyes. Musicians, you know?

Aimi was sitting on a stool near the makeup vanity, fixing a broken string on her cello. She was wearing a short black velvet corset dress, striped black and white stockings, and a Victorian top hat with a long black veil that trailed down her back almost to the floor. She looked up at once, her eyes dark and distant, mouth smirking but not smiling. Her makeup was absolutely perfect, as usual, Asian white, with blue lipstick and black vine-like henna scrawled around her eyes and down over her cheeks like tears.

The henna was real. That is, it was permanent, the result of all the slime that had leaked out of the corners of her eyes. Qilin had left his mark on her in so many ways, including the fact that while her father was recuperating in a hospital in Tokyo, she was now more or less responsible for his empire. At present, she was using every resource she had to monitor Qilin, should he ever return. It almost didn't seem fair. So many people had died, so many kids, but Dr. Mura, who had started this whole mess, had managed to be rescued from his smashed car with only minimal injuries to his legs.

I set the thought aside and smiled at her, and she gave me a little wave back. It had become our routine. I would see her at school, in the music room, pass her in the halls, or spot her in the library, and give her a smile. She always smiled back or gave me a wave, but there was a wariness in her eyes when I approached her, and sometimes she shirked unexpectedly when I was standing to close to her, almost like she could sense my Kami and was afraid of it.

I thought about what she had had suffered, what she might suffer again, if Qilin ever re-surfaced. I wanted to believe that Qilin was gone forever, burned away in Raiju's fire—but Qilin, like Raiju, was a god. Can a god ever really die?

Too many of the old Japanese folktales end badly. I want this one to end well. Maybe I'll even get my wish....

"You're late, moron," Snowman barked, throwing a tube of eyeliner at me. He was dressed in a white military suit, complete with standing collar, gold embroidery and epaulettes. He was running his hand through his hair, which was spiked into long white-gold quills that gave him a very distinct Goblin King look. I'm sure he had chosen it just to annoy me. "You're too good to come out and see your crew play now?"

He was giving me dagger eyes, so I gave them right back to him. "I'm here now, dumbass."

He turned away and went to stand in front of the full-length mirror to fix his red satin cravat. This was something new. Snowman never backed down, no matter how much grief I gave him.

"You're really scared?" I said, coming up behind him.

"No," he answered, but his hennaed eyes danced around the walls nervously.

Sigh. Ever since he had learned that reps from all the major music labels would be here tonight he had been pinging off walls in the worse possible ways. Fighting. Being a smartass. Running out of class so he could cry his little mascaraed eyes out in the sink of the washroom. Nightmare stuff. The idiot couldn't seem to grasp that when you sing the way he does, and you do it on the number one news program in the United States, stuff like this was pretty much a given.

Sounds like a dream, right? Every kid's fantasy to be a teen rock star. Yet, somehow or other, Snowman had gotten himself all wound up over it. He kept talking about art and using phrases like "famous for being famous." Musicians. Their egos are waaay too fragile, as far as I'm concerned.

For just about the hundredth time he started talking about his music, how no one seemed to care about that, how nobody understood him, all kinds of hippie-type crap. So I walked up to him, turned him around, and clocked him in the jaw, trying not to mess up his makeup too badly in the process. I knocked him straight to the floor in his shimmering suit, which was pretty damned impressive, if you ask me.

Everyone in the room let out a collective sigh.

Speechless, he stared up at me like he had no idea he had it coming.

I relaxed my fists at my side. Console the crybaby…check. Knock out the crybaby…okay that wasn't on the list, but I was improvising. "I didn't get a chance to freak. I had to go out there and kick monster ass all on my own. I didn't act like a moron!" I shouted back. "Now get up!"

Snowman climbed slowly to his feet, eyes seething in a familiar way. He started to snarl something at me, but the club owner chose that moment to stick his head into the room to inform us the band was on. Snowman gave the owner an innocent smile, telling him that they'd be right there, yadda, yadda, while rubbing his soon-to-be-a-bruised jaw. The second the dressing room door closed he turned to face me, fists clenched, body shaking with rage.

"Are you going to waste energy on me, Snow?" I asked. "Or are you gonna save it for the stage?"

He thought about that. He roared at me in frustration, then stomped off toward the door, his band in tow.

I watched them leave. They were all stifling giggles, even the twins.

Aimi was last to leave, carrying her cello in a coffin-case. She turned around in the doorway and just looked at me, but there was no amusement in her face.

"Good luck with the gig. Break a leg, or whatever," I told her.

I thought she would turn and race to join the others, but she set the case down and ran back to me, suddenly hugging me fiercely. We stayed that way for a long time, her head resting against my chest. Finally, I leaned down and kissed the top of her head. She turned her head upward and said, softly, "Thank you, Kevin. For everything."

In that perfect moment, our mouths touched. I kissed her, really kissed her, as I had wanted to all along, as I had dreamed I would. I slid my hands up her arms to her shoulders and held her as she kissed my mouth and my face all over.

Then she started to squirm.

"Kevin," she mumbled between kisses, "hands."

"Um," I said, "what?"

"Your hands."

I looked at them, recognizing the weird golden aura that usually precipitated them bursting into flaming torches. "Oh," I said, releasing her and stepping back. I shook my hands until the glow faded away. That was probably the worst drawback of being Raiju's Keeper: I couldn't keep the flames down when I got excited. This was definitely going to play havoc with my love life in the future.

Snowman was right; I really was a hothead.

Aimi looked at me and smiled in sympathy. There were no tears, but that didn't mean anything, I reminded myself that she was no longer capable of crying then. "Kevin," she said, her eyes shining, "You're my personal hero." Then she picked up her cello case and hurried out the door.

4

The band did great, but you knew they would, didn't you?

At the end of the performance, while Snowman was still riling the audience, doing that thing onstage that made all the girls in the room swoon, a net was released and hundreds of white paper roses with the fire-gradient Destroyer logo imprinted on them were released into the audience. The club, already full of a low-lying glycol-based, fog-machine mist, took on a fantastic, otherworldly look as everyone exploded with cheers and demands for encores.

The band stood there, smiling and throwing paper flowers. The kids in the club surged forward for autographs, and I saw some of the suited execs moving in, trying to get the band's attention. Someone shouted about an American Idol audition reel, but I didn't hang around.

This was Aimi's night, Destroyer's night. I headed for the exit.

The parking lot was quiet, empty, with a full harvest moon riding high above the city like a giant, blink-less red eye. I shrugged off the chill as I headed for Jennie, waiting patiently for me by the fence. I leaned against the bike, lit a clove with my fingertips, and watched the sky deepen and the stars bleed through in pinpricks of diamond light—maybe like the eyes of the Kami waking up and watching, waiting for a chance to take back their earth.

It made me wonder how many more were out there—Kami, and their Keepers. I wondered what forms they took, and if and when I would encounter any more of them. I wondered if I would have to fight them, or if we couldn't all just try to get along.

After I had smoked the cigarette down to a small nub, I mounted the bike, the finely-tuned engine roaring alive, so loud in my ears I almost didn't hear the alley side door slamming shut. I glanced aside and saw Aimi clopping toward me across the parking lot in her enormous platform boots, still dressed in her performance clothing. Her top hat flew off, but she didn't seem to care.

"Aimi?" I said, surprised she wasn't inside—like Snowman, soaking up all that yummy adoration she and the band had earned. "What are you doing out here?"

She didn't say anything. She just jumped on the back of the bike and wrapped her arms tight around my waist. I tried to ask more questions, but she leaned forward and kissed me on the lips to silence me. She whispered in my ear, "Just ride, handsome."

So we did.

The End

K. H. Koehler is the author of various novels and novellas in the genres of horror, SF, dark fantasy, steampunk and young adult. She is the owner of K.H. Koehler Books, and her books are widely available at all major online distributors. Her covers have appeared on numerous books in many different genres, and her short work has been featured on Horror World, Literary Mayhem, and in the Bram Stoker Award-winning anthology Demons, edited by John Skipp. She lives in the beautiful wilds of Northeast Pennsylvania with two very large and opinionated Rottweilers. She welcomes reviews and fan mail. Visit her website at http://khkoehlerbooks.wordpress.com/